PAYBACK

ALSO BY LEE GOLDBERG

King City
The Walk
Watch Me Die
McGrave
Three Ways to Die
Fast Track

The Ian Ludlow Thrillers
True Fiction
Killer Thriller
Fake Truth

The Eve Ronin Series
Lost Hills
Bone Canyon
Gated Prey
Movieland

The Fox & O'Hare Series (coauthored with Janet Evanovich)
Pros & Cons (novella)
The Shell Game (novella)
The Heist
The Chase
The Job
The Scam
The Pursuit

The Diagnosis Murder Series
The Silent Partner
The Death Merchant

Kill Them All (with Harry Shannon)
The Beast Within (with James Daniels)
Fire & Ice (with Jude Hardin)
Carnival of Death (with Bill Crider)
Freaks Must Die (with Joel Goldman)
Slaves to Evil (with Lisa Klink)
The Midnight Special (with Phoef Sutton)
The Death March (with Christa Faust)
The Black Death (with Aric Davis)
The Killing Floor (with David Tully)
Colder Than Hell (with Anthony Neil Smith)
Evil to Burn (with Lisa Klink)
Streets of Blood (with Barry Napier)
Crucible of Fire (with Mel Odom)
The Dark Need (with Stant Litore)
The Rising Dead (with Stella Green)
Reborn (with Kate Danley, Phoef Sutton, and Lisa Klink)

The Jury Series
Judgment (aka .357 Vigilante #1)
Adjourned (aka .357 Vigilante #2: Make Them Pay)
Payback (aka .357 Vigilante #3: White Wash)
Guilty (aka .357 Vigilante #4: Killstorm)

Nonfiction
The Best TV Shows You Never Saw
Unsold Television Pilots 1955–1989
Television Fast Forward
Science Fiction Filmmaking in the 1980s (cowritten with
William Rabkin, Randy Lofficier, and Jean-Marc Lofficier)
*The Dreamweavers: Interviews with Fantasy
Filmmakers of the 1980s* (cowritten with William
Rabkin, Randy Lofficier, and Jean-Marc Lofficier)
Successful Television Writing (cowritten with William Rabkin)

PAYBACK

LEE GOLDBERG

CUTTING EDGE

Published by
Cutting Edge Books
PO Box 8212
Calabasas, CA 91372
www.cuttingedgebooks.com

*To Bill, my (sometimes) better half, and to
Karen E. Bender, who makes me whole*

PAYBACK

PROLOGUE

Sunday, May 27

S ergeant Ronald Shaw always thought his own death would catch him by surprise, leaving him only a split second to contemplate his doom. He never thought it would be like this.

The black homicide detective lay flat on his back, his legs straight and his arms flush against his sides, as stiff as the wood that imprisoned him. The air was hot and heavy, making him think of the musty wool blanket his mother used to drag out of the attic and put on his bed in the wintertime. He was thinking a lot about the past now, mostly of sunlight and open spaces.

The worst part had been the pain, which sat in the hollow of his empty stomach and seeped, milky and sour, into every vein and capillary of his body. But he gradually accepted it and it stopped being an adversary and became a companion. The enormity of his loneliness was worse than the pain.

His eyes were open wide now, fixed on the tiny shaft of light that fell through the narrow metal pipe and dripped fresh air on his face. It was his only connection to the outside world, a world separated from him by the coffin walls and six feet of dirt.

Shaw had no idea how long he had been buried here nor how much time he had left until it no longer mattered. Sometime ago, he didn't know when, he had come to accept his death, even welcome it. His only fear now, in those rare moments of lucidity between his forceful memories of the past and chilly unconsciousness, was that Brett Macklin would make the fatal mistake of trying to save him.

CHAPTER ONE

Friday, May 18, 10:45 P.M.

W*e're in deep shit.*

That's what twenty-year-old Dennis Vercammen thought, sitting snug and thoroughly buzzed in the white leather back seat of his daddy's custom-made 1981 Eldorado convertible, his arm around Gloria Pensky and his hand cupping her gelatinous left breast. Sandra Muirdoe sat in front of him, shooting worried glances at Reeves Rabkin, who was driving and stomping the gas pedal in a desperate attempt to stop the sputtering engine from dying.

The white convertible glowed like neon in a neighborhood where everything looked black. The beaten gray buildings blurred into the shadows and the streetlights cast a yellowish haze over the roadway that dissipated before reaching the sidewalks.

The car made one last, spasmodic lurch and everyone in the car realized what Dennis already knew.

"We're in deep shit," Sandra muttered.

Reeves glanced over his shoulder at Dennis with wide eyes that said, "This can't be real."

Dennis nodded and looked past Reeves into the shadows. He saw three black youths, with their rigid faces and furious eyes, move off the curb and glide toward the car.

"C'mon Reeves, start the car. This isn't funny," Gloria whined, noticing the three blacks. Dennis felt her heart pounding in his palm and gave her breast a squeeze.

Reeves noticed Gloria and Dennis looking past him and turned in the direction of their gazes.

"Fuck." Reeves eyed the three guys heading toward them. He glanced back at Dennis. "Stay cool and let me handle this."

Dennis shrugged, his head bobbing on his rubbery neck. Drinking made his head feel like someone had ripped open his skull and scooped out the heavier parts of his brain. That was why he let Reeves drive and that was why he gladly accepted Reeves's offer to deal with this. After all, it was Reeves's idea to go to that goddamn frat party at USC and his fucking shortcut to the freeway that got them stuck in this hellhole. So Reeves damn well better handle this.

Dennis could tell the three blacks weren't goodwill ambassadors coming to welcome them into the neighborhood. They were too poor to look hip and too hip to look poor. One guy, perhaps no more than fifteen years old, wearing jeans, blue canvas tennis shoes, and a ratty black leather jacket, stopped at the front of the car and started twisting the hood ornament absently, his eyes licking Sandra's body like a popsicle.

Sandra sank uneasily down in her seat under the teenager's stare. Another guy, with pockmarked cheeks and deep-set, thin eyes and wearing a gray sleeveless sweat shirt that let his muscular arms sway unhindered, strutted around to the passenger side and stood next to Sandra.

"Hey, shouldn't you guys be out there break-dancing or something?" Sandra's voiced cracked. "I'd sure like to see you dudes do a quick moon walk right back where you came from."

The third man laughed, adjusted his reflective sunglasses, and came up beside Reeves. Dennis noticed the deferential way the other two blacks looked at the third man, and assumed he was the leader.

"We've had some engine trouble," Reeves said evenly in a neutral, matter-of-fact tone that was utterly emotionless. Dennis immediately thought of Mr. Spock. "Is there a gas station nearby we can push the car to?"

The guy in the sunglasses ignored Reeves and faced Dennis. "Look, Benny, that asshole is grabbin' the bitch's tit."

"Dennis, let go of Gloria's tits," Reeves said in that same flat tone, without looking back. Dennis didn't respond. He didn't feel like he was there; it seemed like he was watching it all on TV.

Suddenly the pockmarked man next to Sandra thrust his hand into her blouse, grabbing one of her breasts. She shrieked and grabbed his wrist, trying to pull his hand out.

Benny laughed, his hand deep in Sandra's blouse. "I got me some tit too, Luthor." He twisted her breast until she cried out. "Ain't bad neither."

"We don't want any trouble, guys," Reeves said. "We just want to get our car fixed and get out of here, okay?" Dennis expected Reeves to paralyze Luthor with a Vulcan neck pinch.

"Trouble?" Luthor crooned. "What trouble?"

The teenager in front of the car twisted the hood ornament roughly until it snapped off in his hand with a metallic crack. Reeves glared at him. Dennis wasn't too thrilled either. His dad had dished out $20,000 to a Jewish man with buckteeth to fix up the car, to cut off the roof and add a wheel well to the trunk. The flow of cash from Dad into Dennis's pockets might dwindle severely if the car was damaged. And to Reeves that meant there would be less cash to leech off of Dennis, which meant less booze, less coke, and less pussy in Reeves's future.

In short, things were getting serious.

"That's just about enough, boys," Reeves hissed, his face twisted into a snarl. Dennis was surprised. He had never heard Reeves talk that way. Reeves dropped the Mr. Spock bit and was now doing his best Charles Bronson.

"Really?" Luthor asked in a singsong voice.

"You heard me, bro," Reeves said. "Why don't you boys just take a walk."

"Dipshit here is getting mad," Luthor said, glancing at his friends. "He wants us to take a walk. My, my, what should we do?"

The teenager in front of the car whirled, hurling the hood ornament at the windshield. Gloria screamed and everyone in the car dove down as the windshield cracked. Reeves slammed the car door open into Luthor's gut and spilled clumsily out of the car.

Luthor recovered quickly. Before Reeves could stand, Luther jammed two fingers into Reeves's nose and yanked him up. Reeves squealed, blood streaming out of his nostrils and down the back of Luthor's hand. Reeves looked into his reflection in Luthor's sunglasses.

"You think you got balls, huh?" Luthor grunted, suddenly grabbing Reeves's crotch with his free hand and crunching the testicles between his fingers. Reeves screamed, squirming in Luthor's hands. "Don't ya, prickless?"

Luthor laughed. "Hey Benny, ream this asshole's woman so she knows what she's been missin'."

"No!" Sandra yelled.

Benny lifted her effortlessly out of the car and dumped her, kicking and writhing, on the ground at his feet. "Get ready to gargle some manhood, cunt. You're gonna get a third-world tonsillectomy."

"Hey, fellas—" Dennis began. Benny interrupted him with a sobering backhand slap across the face that sent Dennis sprawling onto Gloria.

"Faggot," Benny cackled at Dennis, who lay dazed in Gloria's lap. Then a loud blast rang in Dennis's ear and Benny's head burst apart in an explosion of red froth and gray bits.

Dennis watched in stunned horror as Benny's headless torso stumbled toward him and then toppled over the edge of the car, blood gushing out of his neck and splashing onto the white seats. Dennis knew his dad would never let him borrow the car again.

Dennis looked past Benny's gurgling body and saw a man in a red leather jumpsuit emerge from the darkness across the street, a band of black makeup over his eyes. A New Wave Superman, Dennis thought.

Luthor released Reeves and dashed away into the street, the black teenager running at his side. Reeves crumpled into a heap. The man in red turned toward the fleeing blacks, calmly raised his gun and fired once. The bullet tore into Luthor's back, lifting him up off his feet and tossing him forward. The teenager flinched and kept running.

The gun bucked again in the stranger's hand. The teenager yelped with pain, spun, and fell backward onto the ground.

The man spit and walked past the car without even looking at Dennis or his friends. Reeves reached up, grabbed the car door, and pulled himself to his feet, his eyes on the man walking toward Luthor, who lay motionless in the street.

The man glanced at Luthor's blood-soaked corpse and then crushed Luthor's shattered sunglasses under his heel before stepping over to the groaning teenager. He stopped at the boy's feet and stared down at him. The boy clutched his left leg, blood spraying between his fingers like a small sprinkler.

"I-I'm hurtin' bad," the boy said, trembling.

The man grimaced. "Fucking nigger." He aimed the gun at the boy's stomach and pulled the trigger. Three bullets pounded into the boy in rapid succession, skipping his body across the asphalt.

The man shuffled up to the mangled body, fired one more shot into it, and then walked toward the car, his gun hanging limply at his side.

Reeves curled his lips as if to speak, but he couldn't summon his voice. Sandra whimpered on the ground, thankful yet afraid, careful not to look at the man as he passed. Gloria sat straight up in her seat, staring expressionlessly forward. Dennis watched the man slip back into the night.

"Who are you?" Dennis yelled impulsively.

The man whipped around and Dennis shrank back, half expecting to taste a bullet. The man flashed a cynical grin and pinned Dennis under an icy gaze.

"Mr. Jury."

The sleek, fin-tailed black '59 Cadillac Brett Macklin was so carefully polishing in his garage had almost ended up sticking ass backward out the roof of a seedy Hollywood eatery.

The mean-grilled street shark had suddenly become prized, and woefully misunderstood, Americana. People would gut the cars like fish, junking the powerful V-8, 325-horsepower, 390-cubic-inch engine that gave the '59 Cadillac its bite, slop a few coats of glossy paint on the chassis, and turn it into a bubbling Jacuzzi or mount it on some burger joint.

No one seemed to see the injustice in it except Brett Macklin. The 1959 Cadillac wasn't made to hang above a restaurant door, its twin bullet taillights blinking like Christmas tree ornaments. It was the last American car with balls, with aggressive styling that said "fuck you" and stole the road. Nowadays, Macklin lamented, American-made cars were microscopic bits of tin that farted along roads dominated by boxy foreign cars with high price tags and engines that fit in the glove compartment.

In the three weeks since he outbid a pear-shaped Greek man who wanted to put the car on his West Hollywood falafel hut, Macklin had done nothing but work day and night restoring and modifying it. The exhausting labor kept his mind off the anguish smoldering in his chest.

On a chilly morning less than a month ago, his girlfriend, Cheshire, got into his '59 Cadillac and twisted on the ignition, triggering a bomb that blew her and the car to smithereens in the driveway of his Venice home. The bomb had been meant for him, planted by a gang of psychopathic pedophiles the impotent justice system had failed to punish. Macklin hunted down the killers, as he had the murderers who set his father aflame a year before, and made them pay for their crimes.

Now he was alone again. And angrier than ever before. While restoring the car, he restored himself. Both the car and Macklin were now sophisticated killing machines. Using money and supplies covertly appropriated by Los Angeles Mayor Jed Stocker, Macklin drew on his years as a helicopter designer for Hughes Aircraft and his education in aeronautical engineering to turn the Cadillac into a tank equipped for the urban battlefield.

Macklin was actually bringing the Cadillac back to its spiritual roots. The chassis of the 1959 Cadillac was inspired by the World War II Lockheed P-38 Lightning fighter plane, and now his new, restored "Batmobile" was just as lethal.

First, Macklin made the car nearly impregnable to gunfire. He armored the 221-inch chassis with metal plates, fitted the sloping, teardrop-shaped cab with bulletproof glass, and equipped the car with self-sealing whitewall tires.

Macklin hid a set of strong halogen lamps, designed to blind nighttime pursuers with a burning flash of white light, behind the rocketlike rear grille beneath the sharp fins. But the teeth of the 1959 Cadillac's defensive power lay cloaked behind its menacing front chromework. Two air-cooled .50-caliber machine guns, capable of firing bullets three times as heavy and three times as destructive as .44 Magnum shells, could burst out spitting-hot lead from the centermost of the quadruple headlights.

Macklin stepped back, admiring the car's gleaming black finish, and reached for his can of Michelob on the garage workbench. After being in the stuffy garage throughout the humid evening, Macklin felt like a battered Kentucky Fried Chicken in a pressure cooker.

His white 1984 Olympics T-shirt clung to the damp skin between his shoulder blades and against his sternum. His Levi's cutoffs itched his small buttocks, firmed by years of jogging. The T-shirt was his passing nod to his teenage dream of being an

Olympic-class runner. The dream died but was strong enough to get him through UCLA on a track scholarship.

The remaining three gulps worth of beer were lukewarm, a pleasant reminder of how long and how deeply he had been immersed in his work. He wanted to finish the car in time to drive himself and Shaw to the campaign fundraiser Sunday for black State Assemblyman Cecil Parks, an old friend of theirs running as the Democratic candidate for U.S. Senator.

Humming the Michelob jingle, Macklin strode to the rear, squatted, and pulled a folded sticker from his back pocket. He removed the brown backing and carefully affixed the sticker to the gleaming chrome bumper.

It read: PROTECTED BY SMITH & WESSON.

"You vicious, sadistic bastard!"

Startled by the voice, Macklin jerked his head up and saw Jessica Mordente, a reporter for the *Los Angeles Times,* standing in the doorway leading to his laundry room.

Last time he had seen her, three weeks ago, they were making love upstairs in his bed. They had talked once or twice on the phone since then, but that was it.

She was wearing faded blue jeans and a pink oxford shirt and held a manila envelope under her left arm. Her olive green eyes were wide and glassy, rage tightening her face and forcing the veins and tendons in her neck to bulge against her flushed skin.

"You're Mr. Jury," she shouted, making quick stabs toward him with her finger, "and I'm going to expose you!"

CHAPTER TWO

Macklin rose slowly, an eyebrow cocked, and regarded her with wary curiosity.

"Mr. Jury is dead," he said.

"A lie," she shot back. "A trick to throw the press off the trail. That corpse wasn't the vigilante. You are."

She whipped the manila envelope out from under her arm and waved it at him. "I got this photo from a source at the FBI. They don't care who you are. They think you're a hero. I've kept it a secret because I thought maybe they were right."

She tore open the envelope, pulled out the photograph, and thrust it at him. "This is a picture of you taken by a bank security camera. That's you gunning down a couple of bank robbers last month."

Macklin felt a shiver of apprehension crawl down his back. He took the picture and held it with both hands. There he was, in crisp black and white, his .357 Magnum flashing.

"Your murder spree is over, Macklin," she said vindictively.

He fell back against the car and let go of the picture, letting it float gently to the floor. In a strange way, he felt relieved. He wouldn't have to kill anymore. But his unmasking would mean publicity. The horror that had killed his father and Cheshire, that had turned him into a vigilante, would now inflict the final injustice—the destruction of Cory, his eight-year-old daughter, and Brooke, his ex-wife. Sergeant Ronald Shaw, who strenuously objected to Macklin's vigilante justice but was tied to him nonetheless by years of friendship, would be prosecuted as a willing accomplice. So would Mort Suderson, the ex-LAPD helicopter pilot Macklin hired to work for his charter airline company.

"Don't think about killing me, Macklin," Mordente said with undisguised disgust. "I've already made arrangements with my lawyer in case I suddenly disappear."

Macklin shrugged. "You win. I'm Mr. Jury. Now what?"

"I expose you."

"Then why not just do it? Why come here first?"

Mordente bent over and picked up the photo. "I wanted to see your face. I wanted to know why you became a killer."

"A street gang ambushed my father, doused him with gasoline, and set him on fire," he said. "The law let them go free."

Macklin looked into Mordente's eyes. The hatred was still there, but there was something else. Sadness, perhaps. Or maybe just weariness. He simply wanted her to understand what he had only just begun to realize—that what he was doing on the streets was worth sacrificing himself and, yes, perhaps those he loved.

"You've killed others too," she hissed.

"Psychos. They raped and killed children and filmed it for profit. I stopped them. It was the right thing to do."

"I was beginning to believe that too," she stammered, her lower lip trembling with rage. "I really wanted to believe that. But tonight you went too far. You murdered a fifteen-year-old kid. A child. I let you go and you murdered a kid and reveled in the bloodshed."

Macklin shook his head, his brow wrinkled with confusion. "What?"

"I had that picture of you three weeks ago," she continued, talking to herself now, looking at him without seeing him. "If I had acted on it then, maybe three people would be alive tonight. But I can make damn sure you don't kill anyone else. Tomorrow I write the story that puts you away."

"I didn't kill anyone tonight," Macklin said. Her head snapped up and she glared at him through narrow eyes. "I've been here, waxing my car."

"Christ, Macklin, when does the lying stop, huh?"

"I have nothing to gain by lying now," Macklin said, keeping his voice steady. "I'm telling you I've been here all night."

Mordente ignored his protest and turned her back to him. "You're finished, Macklin."

"So you're going to leave now and write your article," Macklin said. "Tie me up and hang me out to dry."

She stopped, her back to him. "You got it."

"Tell me, Jessie, how are you going to explain the last three weeks?"

She slowly turned around to face him again.

"How are you going to write your way out of knowing the truth and keeping it quiet for so long?" Macklin continued. "How are you going to describe the night we made love?"

"You're inhuman," she hissed.

Macklin shrugged. "I'm innocent. Give me seventy-two hours and I'll prove it."

"No," she said, her eyes narrow and furious. "You'll run."

"Where could I go?" he replied. "If you write your story, you will stop me. But you will also crush my family. For their sake, not mine, I want a chance to prove my innocence. Three days, that's all I ask. If I don't find the impostor, I'll turn myself in to you and tell all." He paused. "Almost all. I won't say a word about our ever meeting before and that you've known the truth for three weeks. Your exposé will appear ethically and journalistically sound, and you might still have a career afterward."

"All right," she muttered through tight lips. "Seventy-two hours." Her voice rose sharply into a shout that slapped him. "A second more and I'll destroy you, Brett Macklin, I promise you that." She turned and stormed into the house.

He listened to her stomping through the house and then, a moment later, heard his front door slam shut.

Macklin slumped against his car and sighed. He had three days to save his life. Who was this impostor? Was he just a vigilante or was there more to it? Where could he find him? The only place he could think to begin his search was where it all began—the dark alleys and grimy, forgotten streets of South Central Los Angeles. The urban jungle.

The crack of splintering wood broke into Macklin's thoughts. He whipped his head around and saw the back door of the garage burst open and slap against the wall. A police officer, his legs spread out and his gun braced in both hands, stood framed in the doorway.

Macklin shifted his gaze and saw another officer, in his crisp blue suit and hat, standing where Mordente had stood just a few minutes ago. The muzzle of the second officer's gun was right in front of Macklin's face.

"You so much as twitch, Macklin," said the cop behind him, "and we'll give you a couple of extra assholes."

It was after midnight when Macklin pulled open the glass door and stepped into the darkened hallway of the Superior Court. The two cops behind him had their guns out.

Their footfalls echoed eerily through the empty, gray tile corridors as they walked in measured steps toward the last courtroom door. The tall oak door was about a half inch ajar when they approached it. Pushing it open slowly, Macklin saw the room was lit only by the moonglow spilling in through the windows and a tiny reading lamp on the judge's bench.

Ex-Superior Court Judge Harlan Fitz sat behind the bench. He wore a white polo shirt with a red sweater tied around his neck by its sleeves. When Macklin entered, Fitz leaned forward on his elbows, his hands supporting his head and flattening his puffy cheeks, which rolled up against his eyes and gave them an Asian slant.

Los Angeles Mayor Jed Stocker stood in the center of the courtroom with a gun trained on Macklin. The Mayor wore a crooked sneer and a gray three-piece suit, the vest unbuttoned and his tie loosened at the collar.

Shaw sat in the jury box, his legs crossed and resting on the wooden partition. The sleeves of his shirt were rolled up past his elbows and his brown corduroy jacket was draped carelessly over the arm of the chair next to him. He acknowledged Macklin's presence with a quick, subdued glance. Not a good sign.

"How melodramatic," Macklin said as he strode into the courtroom toward Stocker. The cops stood stoically in the doorway, looking to Stocker for their next move.

"Just shut the fuck up, Macklin," Stocker barked. The Mayor waved his gun at the cops and said, "I'll take it from here, boys." The cops nodded affirmatively and closed the door.

"Are those two monkeys really cops?" Macklin asked, jerking a thumb over his shoulder.

"*My* cops, Macklin." Stocker met Macklin's gaze and held the gun steady. "They know who runs the city. They know who to listen to and they know when not to ask questions."

Macklin glanced past Stocker to Fitz. The judge wearily beckoned Macklin forward with a subtle backward toss of his head.

"What is this party all about?" Macklin asked.

"You've lost control," Stocker replied, shaking his gun for emphasis. "You've become a psycho—a liability."

"I didn't kill anyone tonight." Macklin cautiously sat on the edge of the prosecutor's table, careful not to spook Stocker, and rested his hands on his knees.

"We didn't say anything about killings," Fitz said in an accusatory tone.

Macklin ignored him. He wasn't ready to tell them about Mordente yet. "All I know is that three guys were killed. I'd like to hear the details."

"Three black gang members were roughing up a couple of white kids who accidentally violated their turf," Stocker explained with a patronizing tone. "A guy toting a three fifty-seven stepped out of nowhere and gunned down the gang members."

"You think I did it," Macklin stated.

Stocker nodded. Shaw sat passively.

"What about you, Ronny, do you think I did it?"

Shaw shrugged. "I'm not sure."

"Then why the hell is this brainless creep pointing a gun at me?" Macklin yelled, looking directly at Stocker.

"You're out of control," Stocker hissed at him, "and that makes you a dangerous man."

"There are some extenuating circumstances," Shaw said. "The Mayor left out the sadistic part. The killer went up to the boy, called him a fucking nigger, and pumped three more bullets into him."

Macklin nodded.

"Everything he did up until that point sounds like your usual style," Shaw said, "except for that. Maybe you've just grown to like killing."

Macklin shook his head disbelievingly. "You're crazy."

"Our mental capabilities aren't in question here," Fitz said. "Yours are. What happened tonight was a massacre. We can't let that happen again."

"Your problem isn't with me. There's a sicko running around out there. He's the one that has to be stopped. We have to find out who he is and why he's killing people." Macklin stood up, crossing Stocker's path. "C'mon, look at this rationally for a moment. I was the one who insisted Judge Fitz become involved, remember? I'm the one who asked for a judicial review of my actions."

Macklin walked up to the jury bench and faced Shaw. "Mr. Jury was dead, Ronny. Why the hell would I resurrect him?"

"Yeah, and what about the death car you've been building in your garage?" Stocker said, a snide smile etching a crooked line across his face. "Is that a recreational vehicle or what?"

Macklin whirled around. "Before you shit through your mouth again, just remember you're the one who forced me into becoming Mr. Jury, and you're not about to let me stop."

"It didn't take a helluva lot of force, Mack," Shaw said. "And you can stop anytime you want. Let's not kid each other. You want to be Mr. Jury. I realized that a long time ago. So don't act so goddamn self-righteous."

Macklin sighed wearily. "We're just going around in circles. I didn't kill them. Granted, it was the sort of situation I might have stepped into and cleaned up, but I certainly wouldn't slaughter a defenseless kid."

He turned back to Shaw. "And I wouldn't call him a fucking nigger. We all know I'm not a racist. Besides, if I had become a blood-crazed lunatic, I don't think I'd be here now arguing with you."

"Unless you were afraid we'd stop you from having your grisly fun," Stocker said.

"Stocker, I'd shine the toe of my shoe with your scrotum right now if I didn't think that would support your stupid allegations."

"That's enough," Fitz declared. "Put that gun away, Stocker."

Stocker hesitated, glaring at Macklin.

"*Now,*" Fitz said.

Stocker reluctantly slid the gun into his waistband.

"I think Macklin deserves the benefit of the doubt," Fitz said. At least *someone* believes me, Macklin thought.

Shaw chuckled derisively. "I can't believe what I'm hearing. You're all ignoring the implications of this. Can't you see what this vigilante lunacy has finally come to? If Mack didn't do it tonight, someone else did. Other people may jump on the meat wagon too. The Mr. Jury we've created has become the justification psychos need to butcher people."

"Don't dump those bodies on my doorstep. Don't blame me for the actions of crackpots and psychos," Macklin said. "They don't need any justification for their actions. They could use Mr. Jury, or Jesus, for justification, it makes no difference."

"Where do you draw the line between good murder and bad murder? You're both killing people," Shaw responded.

"That's like asking what's the difference between Hitler's Nazis and the soldiers who hit the beaches at Normandy," Macklin said. "In this country we have a system of law; we don't have a system of justice. Violent crime is running rampant in this city and I'm doing something about it. Every day that these murderers roam the streets, your family and mine are in danger. I've never killed an innocent person."

"Yet," Shaw said.

"That's all irrelevant right now, gentlemen," Fitz said solemnly. "We've got a sadistic killer on our hands, calling himself Mr. Jury."

"And while we're in here sitting on our asses, he's still on the streets." Macklin approached the judge's bench, feeling Stocker's insolent glare against his back. "I'd like to do something about it."

Fitz didn't hesitate. "Get him."

CHAPTER THREE

Saturday, May 19, 11:53 A.M.

The single-story, white wood-frame house sat on a granite point overlooking the shimmering blue lake. The triangular aluminum roof reflected the sun's rays beaming down from a cloudless sky into Jessica Mordente's eyes as her car bounced along the fifty yards of unpaved roadway leading to the house.

A tall guard tower flanked each side of the cyclone gate in front of her, the only opening in the two parallel electrified fences that circled the tree-studded mile around the private lake. A single man, a rifle slung over his shoulder, stood like a life-size plastic GI Joe doll in each of the two thirty-foot-tall stations. In the gap between the fences, expressionless men in brown fatigues walked at a marchlike clip and, like the dogs at their sides, seemed to snarl instead of breathe. The guards probably lifted their legs to pee too, she thought.

The gate in front of her parted just wide enough to let one of the guards pass through. She slowed her Mazda RX-7 to a stop six yards short of the gate and rolled down her window.

The guard had a long snout and a butch salt-and-pepper crew cut. He licked his lips with his pink tongue as he rounded the front of her car. She wondered if she'd have to offer him a doggie treat to get him to speak. She'd rather ask him to roll over and play dead and just let her drive through.

"My name's Jessica Mordente," she said, all smiles. "I have an appointment to interview Anton Damon."

The guard grunted, which was a more literate response than Mordente had expected, and walked in a leisurely way to the gate again. He picked up a military-issue walkie-talkie and spoke into it. She saw him nod at the men in the guard tower.

The gate swept open toward her with an electric whine. She put the Mazda in gear and drove forward. The guard immediately raised his hand, palm out, and she stopped. She watched as a fourth guard emerged from behind one of the towers and walked to her car with the snout-faced man.

"We have to search your car," the snout-faced man said.

Mordente had expected it, but that didn't make her any happier about it. She rose from the car, her purse slung over her shoulder. "Sure. While you're poking around in there, could you empty the ashtrays and vacuum a bit too?"

The guard gave no indication that he had even heard her. "Your purse," he said.

She took the purse from her shoulder and handed it to him. He unzipped it and dumped the contents out on her hood. Mordente lunged for two canisters of lipstick and a couple of tampons before they could roll off the sloping hood. When she straightened up, she saw that both guards had their guns out.

Mordente carefully set the lipstick and tampons on the hood and stepped back. "Take it easy, boys. I'm not going to gloss your lips and shove tampons down your throats."

The guards faced her motionlessly for a long moment and then holstered their guns. While the snout-faced man examined her microcassette recorder, wallet, creased reporter's notebook, and assorted crap, the other leaned into the passenger side of her car and clawed and sniffed around the interior. He tossed out a half-empty can of Pepsi Free and an Egg McMuffin container.

Mordente sighed and turned her back to them to give the compound the once-over while they searched her car. The house was white with green trim and had a rustic, woodsy look about it that suggested it was built by hand by some dedicated woodsman fifty years ago. Then again, she thought, there are a lot of prefab-ricated tract homes that have the same woodsy look.

Take away the mongrel guards and the electric fences, and the place could be a summer camp. It could also be a cozy lake-side resort where families could relax and get away from the crush of urban life in smog-shrouded Los Angeles, which was down the mountain and sixty-five miles northwest. It seemed wrong that such a warm place was home for such a cold organi-zation. This was White Wash Group territory; no dark-skinned individuals allowed.

"Hey," the guard snapped. She turned and saw him hold-ing a small metal detector. He jerked the detector to motion her toward him. Mordente shuffled to his side and he ran the metal detector over her body. At least he didn't try a strip search, she thought.

"All right, you can drive through," the guard said, click-ing off the detector. "Slowly," he drawled. Mordente shrugged and took her purse from him. To her surprise, everything had been neatly put back, tampons and all. She wondered if he had sharpened her pencils too. Mordente got into her car and drove through the gate.

As she wound around to the front of the house, Damon emerged and stood on the porch, right beside the short American flag that jutted in a jaunty salute from one of the green posts. She stopped the car and studied him through the passenger window for a moment. Damon's wide hips and thin legs were held tight in a pair of blue Generra jeans, the front pockets bulging with what looked like marbles. His short-sleeved, cream-colored shirt had epaulets on the shoulders and was unbuttoned all the way from the loose strands of gray hair on his sun-pinkened chest to the dimin-utive, asterisklike navel in the center of his bloated belly. Twelve years of prison life had plumped him up like a Ballpark frank.

Mordente reached into her purse and clicked on the recorder. She pulled the purse strap over shoulder, rose from the car, and immediately exuded her brand of reporter friendliness, not unlike the forced buoyancy of an airline stewardess. She was all smiles as she met him on the porch, which was covered with a fine layer of brittle pine needles.

"Expecting a war to break out?" Mordente asked, shaking his outstretched hand. His squeeze was tentative but firm, and he met her question with an amused smile. His teeth were bone white and perfectly straight. She was uncomfortably aware of his eyes lingering on her sweat-moistened cleavage, slightly exposed by the open collar of her white, short-sleeved blouse, and resisted the urge to cover herself with her hand.

"Depends on what you mean. Am I on the defensive from direct, frontal assaults like the one you just mounted or from an armed offensive against those gates?" He grinned affably and shrugged as he stepped off the porch to her side. "I'd have to say both."

He slid his arm around her shoulder and led her around the house toward the lake. His arm felt like a heavy, damp hose draped around her neck. She knew he was sneaking sideways glances down the opening of her shirt.

Mordente stepped aside, smiling as she politely shrugged the arm off her shoulder. He didn't seem to notice and continued walking.

"As you know, there are many people who are violently opposed to my earned freedom," he said. "The guards make me feel secure."

"But isn't all this weaponry a blatant violation of your parole?" she asked incredulously. The guards pacing along the sandy shore ahead gave the two a wide berth as Damon led her toward a small dock stretching out into the lake.

"I am merely a guest here," Damon said. The sparkle in his eyes was reminiscent of the fiery young Damon, the charismatic man who brought the white supremacists he led to national attention during the middle-class upheaval of the late sixties and early seventies. "The lake belongs to Justin Threllkiss, and the guards are in his employ."

She paused to take off her white leather pumps before trudging across the sand. She knew Threllkiss; most L.A. reporters did. The eighty-three-year-old industrialist and archconservative was always good for a headline-grabbing quote or two about the inferiority of Jews, homosexuals, Mexicans, women, and, most of all, blacks. Threllkiss's gnarled, squat body, pale, freckled skin, and thick, tortoiseshell glasses made him appear to all the world like a harmless eccentric made senile by time and conservative by wealth. Articles about him were given the same serious consideration readers gave Broom Hilda and The Wizard of ID.

Mordente and Damon trudged silently across the sand to the dock, her mind still on Threllkiss. She was wary of Threllkiss's infirm, elderly persona. Threllkiss's multinational oil, construction, and chemical corporations were among the world's largest, and he was still very much in control, directing them all while he scooted around his private Palm Springs golf course in a customized cart larger than some midsize sedans.

He had groomed his son to take over, but he was killed a decade ago in a helicopter crash. Now all Threllkiss had under his thumb was his grandson, a nervous twenty-three-year-old with a taste for PCP, Marilyn Chambers movies, and Hollywood parties thrown by local Republicans.

So the White Wash became Threllkiss's paternal interest. Threllkiss was the financial heart that pumped life into the White Wash, even when most thought the cult was dead and buried.

"You, of course, are the only one who knows I'm here," Damon said, leading her onto the dock. "I trust you have stuck to the agreement my lawyers reached with your publisher."

"Of course," she said. "Your location is still a secret."

"Good," he said. "You know how nasty those civil rights activists can get."

Mordente sighed inwardly but kept her face impassive.

The dock's wooden planks groaned under the weight of their footsteps. A twelve-foot-long aluminum barge rocked on the lake's tiny swells, bouncing against the side of the dock. Four foam rubber boat pillows covered in colored plastic had been tossed haphazardly on the boat's three benches amid a clutter of fishing tackle.

Mordente shrugged. "The people who protested your release believed that you volunteered for the bone marrow transplant with that ill Jewish child as a blatant parole ploy," she said. "And no one has forgotten the Kallahan slaughter that put you behind bars in the first place."

Damon held the palms of his hands out in front of him and gave her a Santa Clausian guffaw comprised of three quick HO, HO, HOs. "Now, that's a loaded remark full of leading questions and ill-advised charges. I'll tackle that once we're out on the lake." Damon stepped into the boat and sat on a pillow next to the dirty white outboard motor. She heard the air sigh from the pillow beneath him.

"Out on the lake?" she asked.

He grinned. "This *is* a fishing expedition, isn't it?"

"Cute," she nodded.

His grin didn't waver. "Nothing relaxes me more than still-fishing on a sunny afternoon. You'll enjoy it."

Damon reached his hand out to her. She ignored it and got into the boat on her own, settling down on the center bench. Damon untied the boat and yanked on the cord. The engine roared and churned the water. He looked past Mordente to the open lake and switched the engine from neutral into forward gear.

The boat sliced into the water with a sudden jolt, the bow rearing up. Mordente grasped the rim of the boat to steady herself. Damon looked amused.

The rush of clean mountain air that whipped Mordente's hair was exhilarating after weeks of being trapped in the sludge layer of car exhaust and industrial filth baked by the sweltering heat of Los Angeles. After five minutes of cutting across the lake water, Damon slowed the boat twenty yards shy of the shore opposite Threllkiss's home.

"I know a spot on the lake, an underwater hole, where the trout like to hide," Damon yelled over the grind of the engine. Mordente nodded mutely. Big deal. She had never fished in her life. As far as she was concerned, that was Mrs. Paul's job. She was here to do an interview and not to audition for a spot on *American Sportsman.*

Damon killed the engine and let the boat glide of its forward momentum as he dumped a cement-filled coffee can attached to a rope over the side. He clapped his hands together.

"Now we're all set." Damon lifted up a fishing pole and plucked a five-inch-long night crawler from a jar on the floor. It wiggled between his thumb and forefinger. "You know, when I was in prison I used to dream about fishing—the solitude of it and the freedom, the thrill of feeling the tug of a fish on the line."

Mordente pulled the tape recorder out of her purse and set it on the bench beside her as she watched Damon thread the hook through the head of the night crawler. Yellowish goo spurted out of the worm where he inserted the hook. She looked away, her gaze sweeping over the lush blanket of trees that covered the hills around the lake.

Damon pointed to a light band around a portion of the worm. "You can cut a worm anywhere but here, separate it into a dozen pieces and it will live as a dozen new worms. But break this band and the worm dies. This band is the creature's bond with life."

He pinched the worm apart just below the band and tossed the remainder back in the jar. The hooked worm squirmed, the hook running up the center of its body.

"My dreams weren't enough to fill the emptiness of prison life," he continued. Judging by his paunch, Mordente figured exercise wasn't enough either. "I realized I had to start life anew. I had to go back in time and rebuild my wayward life. I dedicated myself to becoming reborn in mind and born again in spirit through Jesus Christ."

She kept silent. She'd ask her questions later. Right now, he seemed to be doing just fine on his own. Damon, she guessed, liked to hear himself talk.

He handed her the pole. She took it and let the hook tap the surface of the water. She could see the worm wiggling in the water.

"Hit the switch on the reel to release the line and let it drop until it goes slack, then reel it up three times," Damon said, baiting his hook.

She pressed the switch with her thumb. The hook dropped into the water and line spilled out of the reel. Looking over her shoulder, she could see a guard on the nearest shore spying on them with binoculars.

His own line baited, Damon faced the water and let his line fall over the side of the boat. When his line curled slack, he reeled it up until it was taut.

Damon sighed, pulled a handful of peanuts from his bulging pocket, and popped two, shell and all, into his mouth.

"So, Ms. Mordente," he said, crunching on his peanuts, "I suppose you'd like me to talk about those people I dismembered."

CHAPTER FOUR

He didn't look like the same Anton Damon who had butchered Dr. Martin Kallahan, his wife, Emma, and their nineteen-year-old daughter, Angela, on that muggy afternoon in 1968. He didn't look like the man who chopped them into pieces with an ax and scattered their remains over a dry riverbed.

Kallahan was the first black University of California chancellor, a man who encouraged the sort of minority achievement the White Wash abhorred. Damon took it upon himself to correct that.

The nation was captivated by his sensational murder trial. It was a Damon tour-de-force. He sat in the courtroom like a bird of prey perched on a sharp ledge, with his legs drawn against his chest, his head resting on his knees, and his intense eyes trained on the judge. Damon's outbursts were sudden and vicious. He would hiss insults at witnesses, launch into passionate speeches about racial inferiority, and, as he did twice, leap on the defense table and try to piss on the judge.

The Anton Damon that was forever emblazoned in Jessica Mordente's mind was the defiant, sweat-dampened face that stared back at her from the cover of *Newsweek* magazine, the eyes that dared you to read the stark white type in the banner headline across his chest:

GUILTY!

This Anton Damon munching peanuts in the boat seemed like a different person. Gone was the intensity, the violence, the hate that had oozed from every pore.

"I'm not the same man," said Damon. It was as if he had read Mordente's mind.

"No? What's different?" Mordente asked. "While in prison, you wrote *Supremacy,* and the doctrine preached in those pages differs little from the doctrine of your White Wash days. You still seem to believe that inferior human beings, mainly blacks, gays, and Jews, are unjustly obtaining positions of social power over superior whites in order to destroy white civilization. You still believe they must be stopped."

"I don't advocate violence. Once I did. I've learned the value of human life," Damon replied, shoving another handful of peanuts into his mouth. His chewing sounded like someone stomping on gravel. "Most importantly, I've found Jesus and redemption through Him. I'm a new person." He crammed two fingers into his mouth and searched for a sliver of peanut shell that was jabbing his cheek. Mordente tried to remember if those were the same two fingers that had impaled the night crawler on the hook.

"And what about the Kallahans? You *did* murder them."

He flicked the shell particle into the lake and wiped his mouth across the back of his wrist. "All men have sinned and fallen short of the glory of God," Damon sighed. "*I* have sinned more than most. But the only sin that is not forgiven is the sin of blasphemy against the Holy Spirit. Any other sin, including murder, including the vile mass murders for which I do repent, can be forgiven and is forgiven."

Without warning, a triumphant bellow erupted from Damon's throat and he yanked his pole back toward him. Mordente jerked with surprise and nearly dropped her own pole into the lake. Damon began reeling quickly. The reel buzzed electrically, sounding like a swarm of bees as it dragged in the thirty-five feet of ten-pound test line. Mordente stood still, her gaze fixed on Damon's face. She recognized his expression now as the same crazed one she had seen on the cover of *Newsweek*.

"Come on, come on," Damon urged, his eyes aglow, his face flushed.

She heard a splash and shifted her eyes to the water. A fish danced on its tail fin along the top of the water, trying to break free. Damon brought the line in steadily.

"It's a two-footer. Look at that, a two-footer," Damon boasted. She was watching his face, ignoring the action on his line. He reached for the net with his right hand and thrust it into the air under the fish. Capturing it in his net, Damon brought the fish into the boat.

"Damn, it's a two-footer all right," Damon said. "A beautiful rainbow. I'll let you take it back, Ms. Mordente. They're good eating."

Mordente felt the interview slipping away. Luckily, the agreement his lawyers struck with her publisher was for two separate interviews. She knew now she'd need them. But before this interview was lost, she wanted to catch him off guard.

"You still believe blacks are inferior, don't you?"

He responded as if the question fell into the natural course of their conversation. He took it in stride.

"My beliefs are irrelevant in the light of God's indisputable truths." Damon pulled a long knife out of his shoe-box-size plastic tackle box with one hand and picked the fish up by the gills with the other. The fish convulsed madly in his hand. "Blacks, it has been proven, are genetic mutations weakening the human species. The trend toward racial integration does not bode well for the future strength of Christian society."

Damon jammed the knife into the fish's belly and sliced up toward the gills. Blood spilled out of the fish's gut and painted Damon's arm in dozens of creeping crimson stripes.

Mordente swallowed, her throat dry. The fish was still alive, squirming and splashing its blood on Damon's shirt in tiny specks.

"You have to bleed them," Damon said, regarding the fish and giving it a disgusted scowl, "or they rot." He dropped the knife, yanked out the fish's organs, and tossed them over his shoulder into the water.

"We, as Christians battling the forces of Satan, are severely outnumbered by the forces of disbelievers." Damon opened the Styrofoam icebox, twisted the hook out of the fish's mouth, and dropped the fish onto the block of blue ice. He stared at it a moment. Mordente could see the fish's gills were working as if trying to suck the moisture out of the air.

"Stupid things. You tear out their guts and yet they still aren't smart enough to know when they're dead." Damon looked up at her. "Oh, yes. Anyway, if you use simple mathematics and combine the number of Jews, Moslems, Buddhists, Hindus—not to mention the pagan cultures of the American Indian and African tribesman—you can see that the minions of Satan far outnumber the followers of the Lord."

Damon leaned over, splashed lake water on his hands, and washed the blood off his arm. "However," he continued, "Jesus says fear not, little flock, for he is our good shepherd and the ravenous wolves will be powerless to render any harm to those of us who recognize him as our Lord, our Saviour, and our commander in the never-ending battle against those who would turn the cross upside down."

"Doesn't Jesus also say love your enemy?" Mordente asked.

"But I do, Ms. Mordente." Damon, eager to get his line back in the water, quickly stuck another worm on his hook. "I love them so very, very much. That's why I don't want to see them harmed by misplacement in society. To make someone live in a way contrary to their nature is the greatest injustice you can inflict." Damon was about to drop his line in the water when he froze, intently watching Mordente's pole.

"What weighed most in the parole board's mind was not your history as a model prisoner nor your renewed devotion to religion. It was, they say, your willingness to volunteer for an extremely dangerous bone marrow transplant to save the life of a Jewish girl," Mordente said. "Why? You must admit it seems contrary to your doctrine."

"I brought a lot of pain and misery to society. The least I could do was undertake one unselfish act that might help an innocent child." Damon nodded toward Mordente's pole. She followed his gaze. The end of her pole bobbed madly toward the water.

"I think you've caught something," he grinned.

Damon entered the house as Mordente's RX-7 bounced back along the roadway toward the gate. Two fish were on ice in the Styrofoam cooler on her passenger seat. He figured the suffocatingly dense heat in the car would melt the ice by the time she was down the hill. Soon the car would smell like a trawler, the fishy stench clinging to her body like a lustful drunk.

"How *did* you rationalize giving your marrow to a Jew?" asked the stocky man at the dining room table, removing a set of headphones from his ears and setting them on the listening device in front of him.

Damon shrugged indifferently. "One step back, two steps forward."

Saturday evening, 11:37 P.M.

His hard-on strained against his red leather jumpsuit toward the jiggling ass that bounced up the stairs in front of him. The stairwell had the acrid stench of urine, the wails of hungry babies echoed down the halls, and the wallpaper was peeling off in ragged sheets that exposed the mouse-size cockroaches scurrying along the decaying wooden framework.

The black whore in front of him was oblivious to it all. The tiresome responsibilities of the business at hand and a life spent in this familiar terrain shut out the environment. Her world for the next fifteen minutes would be the loser in the bullshit outfit trudging up the stairs behind her.

She had only met him a couple of minutes ago, outside the apartment building. "What you 'sposed to be? Huh? Halloween ain't happenin' yet, honey," she had told him when he approached her on the street, the $20 bill balled up in his hand like a wad of used Kleenex. "Sado" was written all over this wimp, dressed up like some kind of funky Batman, utility belt and all. She figured she was in for a slap or two and then a quick, puny ejaculation. Five minutes, tops.

Behind her now, the sound of him lustily dragging in the air as he climbed the stairs was like the ragged noise a dull saw blade makes against wood.

His eyes, jade oracles in a raccoonish dark band of makeup, took in her body. Her buttock-hugging, black polyester mini-dress accented the garters that held her red lace stockings over her rippling thighs. The dress was cut low down her sway back, clear to the dark mole that rested atop the curve to her jaunty rear. She wore black pumps with three-inch heels that thrust her butt up so high he figured a satellite could fly right up her ass. Or, he grinned to himself, my powerful love rocket. She'd like that.

The merchandise, though, the stuff he paid the $20 for, was up front. And he got another look at that as she turned from the stairwell and walked back toward him along the hall. Her gargantuan breasts hung low and unrestrained, swaying lazily from side to side with each step.

When he emerged in the hallway, she had already disappeared into the room, leaving the door open behind her.

He unzipped his jumpsuit as he walked. When he entered the room, she stood facing him, her back to the bed, which was a sunken mattress on a rusted spring frame. The water-stained acoustic tiles on the ceiling were yielding to gravity and threatened to drop at any moment. The double-sashed window was propped open with a brick.

She looked at the pale flesh revealed in the wide V of his open jumpsuit. If it hadn't been for her wealth of anatomical knowledge and the two nearly indiscernible dots of sickly red on either side of his torso, she would never have known it was his chest. She lowered her eyes and saw the red leather cone jutting between his legs. At least, she thought, there was something vaguely manly about this guy.

"You got the biggest cock I ever saw," she intoned wearily. The words sounded as decayed as the room. "I can't wait to feel it inside me."

He closed the door softly behind him and swaggered over to her. Five minutes, tops, she told herself. He put his hands on her shoulders, his penis pressing against her stomach, and peeled her dress down, letting it drop in a heap at her feet. Her breasts were two drooping sandbags hanging from her chest.

His eyes followed her breasts to the rolls of her waist, then down to the tuft of pubic hair fluffing out of her crotchless underwear.

The man pulled down his jumpsuit so that it cupped his testicles and then slammed the palms of his hands against her saucer-size nipples, making her tumble backward onto the bed. As her body hit the solid mattress, he watched her breasts bounce and then sag to her sides.

"Nigger," he hissed.

She stared up at him. One of those slave masters, she thought, fear tickling her between the shoulder blades. They were always the worst.

He dropped on top of her and jammed himself into her, delighting in the way her body buckled defensively. His thrusts began immediately, hard and fast, his breathing locomotive.

She expected him to come in an instant. He didn't. His body twisted and squirmed with each thrust. She raked his back with her fingers, going through the motions of faking pleasure, surprised at the tremendous perspiration that already soaked his skin.

He was pleasurably aware of the frenzy he was working himself up to. His penis was a spear plunging deep into the heart of this wretched species, conquering and subjugating it. Each thrust gave him more power, each thrust struck deeper and deeper into its heathen soul. His manhood, his strength, his overpowering physicality would beat them all.

No one had ever pounded her like this. No one had ever been so totally consumed. It hurt bad between her legs, and her eyes were closed tightly against the pain, her body rocking against his thrusts. She was afraid to stop him. Better to wait for the inevitable end and have Horace, her pimp, beat the shit out of him later.

His reward was growing. The once distant sensation was now running down his back and into his pelvis, expanding. He plunged farther and farther into that subhuman soul, harder and harder. A blinding, beautiful white light burst in his head and covered his body in its soothing glow. He gritted his teeth and stiffened as the light ebbed. His eyes fluttered open.

He looked down at the whore. Her teeth were clenched, her chin high, and the tendons in her neck tensed. She looked down her face and into his eyes. She thought she was staring into a corpse. His colorless lips curved into a coldly maniacal grin as he reached back to his belt with one hand. She followed the hand and saw the glint of clean steel.

"No!" she whispered huskily.

Jerking back his pelvis, he pulled his penis out of her. And jammed the knife in.

CHAPTER FIVE

Sunday, May 20, 5:03 A.M.

The air was still. The smoky brown haze that hung over the city glowed as the sun crept reluctantly into the sky. The mechanical hum of Brett Macklin's Cadillac was the only sound on the street. The buildings loomed lifeless and dull three stories high on either side of him. A drunk disappeared down an alley like a rodent scurrying into the crevice between two boulders.

Brett Macklin watched the sun burn through the night the same way he had watched the day bleed into darkness twelve hours before. The passage of time, which he spent driving endlessly through the maze of South Central Los Angeles streets, had changed nothing for him.

His impostor was still out there somewhere.

Macklin eased the car to a stop at the curb and stared at the asphalt on the street. Three red splashes. The errant drops of red from some unseen painter's giant brush. Here was where the impostor had emerged from the darkness to take three lives and plunge Macklin's life into an abyss. Macklin was no closer to finding the son of a bitch than he was twelve hours ago.

Only a handful of hours, he knew, remained before Mordente exposed him—and Cory and Brooke were destroyed.

He tapped the dashboard nervously with his right hand. Cory and Brooke, he thought. Cory and Brooke. He saw it as it once was, in his Venice house, when they were a family, before the arguing, before the coldness, before they left and Macklin was alone.

Macklin pressed on the gas, screeched across the street in a sharp U-turn, and headed north. He wanted to see them once more, before Monday, before they hated him too much to ever see him again.

Sunday, 8:12 A.M.

The mattress was a blood-soaked sponge under the black prostitute's splayed body. Shaw approached the bed slowly, feeling the three Winchell's doughnuts he ate an hour ago churning in his stomach. Her body reflected her killer's murderous frenzy. A net of deep, jagged slashes crisscrossed her torso and her thighs were totally obscured by grotesque lumps of clotted blood, matted pubic hair, and torn flesh.

"Her name's Anita." Vice Sergeant Sage Mitchell, clad in his favorite checkered polyester sports coat, took a deep drag on his Marlboro and exhaled the smoke through his nostrils. "I've picked her up dozens of times for whoring and dealing along this block."

Shaw glanced at her face. Her eyes were stark, white ovals wide with terror. "Didn't anyone hear anything?"

Mitchell shrugged. "Sure they did."

"No one called the police?"

Mitchell chortled. "C'mon, Shaw, be serious."

Shaw scratched his brow nervously. He felt an irrational urge to reach out and strangle Mitchell and didn't quite know why. The man was just going through the motions of his job and that's all he expected Shaw to do, no more and no less. After all, both of them knew Anita's murder would never be solved. Why waste any effort?

Shaw understood that, he really did. Anita was anonymous, part of the flotsam swirling in the stormy undercurrents of the streets. Occasionally, some of the flotsam washed up on blood-soaked mattresses in fleabag hotels, in rusted garbage bins in forgotten alleys, or crumpled in heaps amid the weeds in a vacant lot.

Shaw hated the role he had to play whenever he faced a corpse like Anita's. It made him feel like a glorified garbage man, making sure bodies get zipped into bags and hauled away before they get smelly and bothersome. Taxpayers didn't give a damn who made the mess as long as it got cleaned up. The thing that made Shaw angry was that Mitchell accepted it all so naturally.

"Did anyone see the guy she came in with?" Shaw asked.

"Yeah, some kinky asshole in a red jumpsuit."

A shiver rippled down Shaw's back. "Red jumpsuit?"

"Yeah, and he had this black shit, makeup or something, across his eyes," Mitchell said. "A real wacko, by the sound of it."

Shaw's heart pounded in his chest. The same man who killed those black youths had butchered this black prostitute. It couldn't be a copycat killing because the police hadn't released to the press that the Mr. Jury who shot the black youths wore a red jumpsuit.

Fear tinged with guilt colored Shaw's thoughts. He had been too hard on his friend Brett Macklin. Mack was right. A maniac was on the loose.

"Watch me, Daddy. Watch me," Cory yelled as she stood shivering wet on the edge of the diving board. She had the peanut-shaped pool at the apartment complex to herself. "I'm gonna dive now. Watch me."

"I'm watching," replied Brett Macklin, shifting the Sunday *Los Angeles Times,* two pounds of unread newsprint, from his sweat-dampened bare legs to the ground between his chaise lounge and Brooke's.

Cory smiled and took a deep breath. "Okay, I'm gonna go!" She bent over tentatively, stretched out her arms, and then tumbled into the water in a nearly fetal position.

Within a second she burst up through the surface, shaking her head and spitting water. "How'd I do, Daddy?"

Macklin grinned. "Just great, honey. Next time try to be straighter, like an arrow." He glanced to his left at Brooke, his ex-wife, her face alight with an amused smile. Sitting so close to her, he could smell the coconut oil that made her copper skin, amply revealed by her skimpy white bikini, so slick and shiny. Sweat beaded on her sharp cheekbones and above her full, scarlet lips. Macklin felt the old desire percolating. Brooke's allure hadn't waned; Macklin had caught several men around the pool sneaking furtive glances at her.

"She sure loves to see you, Brett," Brooke remarked softly. "Just look at how charged she gets." She regarded him solemnly. He sat shirtless in his swimsuit, watching with bloodshot, tired eyes as Cory climbed out of the pool. "You used to see her every weekend. Now months can go by. She thinks it's something she's doing wrong."

"I'm going to dive again, Daddy," Cory announced excitedly, marching to the end of the diving board.

Macklin smiled and nodded. "Go ahead, we're watching."

"You've been a real bastard," Brooke hissed out of the side of her smile. "You've changed."

Brooke was right.

He watched his daughter dive and splash into the water and felt the muscles tighten anxiously in his chest. Macklin loved Cory but was afraid to see her, afraid the violence that seemed to stalk him would get her.

This morning he simply showed up unannounced at their apartment. Cory was overjoyed when he showed up at their front door this morning. She jumped into Macklins arms, and he gave her a tight hug that nearly brought tears to his eyes.

Macklin watched now as Cory swam to the pool's edge and lifted herself out of the water.

"Are you going to disappear again and break her heart?" Brooke said, regarding him carefully. His chest was hard and covered with droplets of sweat. "Because if you are, Brett, leave right now."

Macklin swallowed, his throat dry. Conflicting compulsions waged war inside him. He wanted to grab them both in his arms and run away someplace. He wanted to tell them about his vigilantism before the *Los Angeles Times* could. He wanted to hide, melt into the air, and become invisible. He wanted to tell Brooke he still loved her. He wanted to scream with frustration until his lungs burst. He wanted to bring back his father and start over.

He wanted to be happy again.

"It's been a rough time for me," Macklin said, sorry he had come this morning. Now he realized it would just make things worse. "Dad's murder was a big shock. I had barely gotten over that when Cheshire was killed. My world keeps doing somersaults. I'm not ready to bring Cory and you back into that world yet. Until I can settle things down, both of you will have to be patient with me."

"Here I go!" Cory yelled, vaulting off the diving board. Her straight little body sliced smoothly into the water.

Brooke sighed. "Want to do me a favor?"

"What?"

"You try explaining *that* to her."

Macklin left Brooke and Cory at five-thirty that evening, feeling worse than he had the night before. Seeing them made the doom he faced even more frightening.

He hadn't been able to explain anything to Cory and ended up making vague promises to see her soon. Macklin could feel Brooke's scornful gaze burning into his back as he left the apartment. She had every right to be pissed. But once she knew what he had been doing the last few months, Macklin was sure she would be thankful he had stayed out of their lives.

Macklin had wanted to spend his last evening as a free man with them but couldn't handle the oppressive guilt he felt every time he looked at their faces. He fought the urge to once again aimlessly roam the streets in a ridiculous search for the phony Mr. Jury. Tonight, he decided, he wanted to spend his time with friends. In Macklin's glove compartment there were two tickets to Senatorial-hopeful Cecil Parks's fundraising dinner, and he was going to use them.

7:00 P.M.

The New Horizons Hotel, which everyone simply called "The Arrow," had given Los Angeles the stunning architectural landmark the downtown high-rise district desperately needed. It rose, gleaming, from the shadow of the downtown skyscrapers as Macklin drove toward it.

The hotel looked like two giant staircases back to back, a pyramid with two graduated faces. Interesting, but hardly striking. What set the hotel apart was the arrow of cement, steel, and glass that shot out of the twenty-fifth floor. Though quite solid, the five-story shaft that peaked with a four-level black triangle had a sense of motion to it. To Macklin, it looked like the arrow was soaring toward the stars.

A bright neon glow spilled out into the night from the lobby's covered entranceway. Macklin eased his shiny Cadillac to a stop at the front door. A broad-shouldered black man with a gray mustache and wearing a red top hat and tails, opened Macklin's door, smiled warmly, and held out his hand for the key.

"I haven't seen a car like this in twenty years," the doorman said enviously. "It's stunning, sir. A damn shame they don't make them like this anymore."

Macklin grinned and emerged from the car in a simple black tuxedo with a ruffleless shirt. The doorman's eyes were taking in the car with honest appreciation.

"It's a beautiful dinosaur, all right," Macklin said, slipping his keys and a crisp $20 bill into the doorman's chubby palm. "Take good care of her for me."

"I will, sir." The doorman nodded reverently, gesturing away an approaching teenage carhop wearing an ill-fitting white suit. "It will be waiting for you right here."

As Macklin walked toward the lobby, he looked back as the smiling doorman slowly lowered himself into the driver's seat and firmly grasped the wheel. The lights above Macklin were so bright that he couldn't see anything in the blackness of the street beyond his car.

Macklin tried to shrug away the itchy irritation of the suit against his sunburned shoulders as the lobby doors slid open with a whisper and he strolled into the cool air-conditioned lobby. He faced a clear wall behind which three glass elevators ascended and descended along the center of the hotel to the restaurant, bar, observation deck, and ballroom housed in the arrowhead twenty-five stories up.

One of the elevator doors parted and Macklin saw a familiar face. It was Kirk Jeffries, once his roommate at UCLA, now one of the highest paid political pollsters in the nation.

"Holy shit, you wore a tux!" boomed Kirk Jeffries in a voice almost as loud as his clothing. "Knowing you, I thought you'd show up in a fucking T-shirt and jeans."

Jeffries wore a bright blue, crushed velvet tuxedo with black trim, three four-inch cigars wrapped in cellophane sticking out of his pocket. Blue-trimmed white ruffles spilled out of the opening of his jacket, which barely contained the bulk of his belly.

Macklin felt a broad grin stretch across his face and his chest swell with warmth. He was glad he came. Jeffries limped out of the elevator and grabbed him in a hearty bear hug.

The pollster clapped him solidly on the back. "It's good to see you."

Macklin pulled back and regarded his friend. "How's your arm and leg?"

Jeffries waved a hand in front of Macklin's face. "Shit, the doctor finally got a welder, a blowtorch, some steel and put them back together just fine."

"Have you been able to get Cecil's campaign back on track?" Macklin asked. He knew Jeffries well enough not to be fooled by his sloppy manner. Jeffries was a wizard at manipulating poll and survey results to a candidate's benefit. Once Jeffries had segmented the populace, he could hone a candidate's delivery and bring in the right votes.

Jeffries slipped his arm around Macklin's shoulder and led him to the bank of elevators. "Reworking Cecil's campaign has been like a paid vacation. I'll tell you, though, Cecil got hold of me just in time. I'll make him Senator just like I made him the first black student body president back when all of us were at UCLA."

Macklin could tell by the heavy weight on his shoulder that Jeffries's leg was a bigger handicap than he let on. The elevator doors parted in the middle and they stepped into the bullet-shaped glass capsule. The elevator lifted with a jolt and quickly rose through the roof of the lobby, offering Macklin and Jeffries a sweeping view of Los Angeles, a vast grid of sparkling lights spread out below him.

A glass elevator whooshed down past them, startling Jeffries and Macklin. "Christ, they come close," Macklin said. He looked down and saw that the elevator had stopped at a floor below them.

"This middle elevator is an express straight to the top. It doesn't stop at any of the hotel floors," Jeffries explained.

Macklin could now follow the trail of lights flowing onto Santa Monica Freeway clear to the ocean. He saw the glittering Century City towers to his far left and the tiny dots of lights from the homes that clung to the sharp faces of the Hollywood Hills to his right.

They were suddenly enveloped in blackness as the elevator pierced the arrowhead. The doors slid open at level one, the ballroom.

Macklin ambled slowly out of the elevator and scanned the room. The window-lined ballroom was filled with hundreds of people sitting at round, white-cloth-covered tables with flower arrangements in the center. There was a stage, a dais, and a long white table lined with well-known movie stars and politicians. The clatter of silverware and the low rumble of conversation was inviting. Hanging in the center of the room was a gigantic crystal chandelier that was dwarfed and made insignificant by the beauty and vastness of the twinkling night sky that surrounded everyone.

The two men weaved between the tables toward the front of the room. Macklin spotted Ronny Shaw and his girlfriend, Sunshine, at the table he was being led to. Beyond them, he noticed Mayor Stocker among the celebrities at the table on the stage. He felt the warm feeling that he had been nurturing evaporate. He cursed himself for being so caught up in running away from his fear that he had ignored the fact that Stocker and Shaw would be here. It was as bad as staying with Cory and Brooke tonight would have been. These people were stark reminders that he couldn't run away from tomorrow's fate.

As Jeffries and Macklin neared Shaw's table, Cecil Parks excused himself from a cluster of men he was mingling with and came over to greet them. Jeffries went on to join Shaw and Sunshine.

"Brett!" Parks grinned, giving Macklin a firm handshake with one hand and clapping him on the shoulder with the other. "It's good to see you."

Parks's greatest asset had always been his bright eyes, which radiated friendliness. They were beaming warmly now. He wore a tuxedo identical to Macklin's and had Macklin's same trim jogger's build. Macklin hadn't seen Parks in over a year.

"You still jogging twice a week, Cecil?"

Parks shrugged. "No time, Brett. I do all my running nowadays at banquets and speeches, in interviews and commercials, on fliers and talk shows."

"It's the shits, isn't it?"

"Yeah, but I want to be Senator," Parks said. "Jogging with you and complaining about high defense appropriations, tax credits for schools that racially discriminate, the decay of the Social Security system, and covert government activities in Central America only makes me lose my breath quicker and doesn't change any of it. I want to show that one person can count."

Macklin held up his hands in mock defense. "Okay, okay, you got my vote, Cecil. You can stop your speech now."

They laughed gently until Parks's chuckles waned. "Uh-oh, that oil man married to the movie star with the big tits is looking my way. I'd better go over and schmooze with him. He donated big to my campaign." Parks slapped Macklin's shoulder again. "Hey, Brett, let's not be strangers, okay? I miss those talks we had when we jogged together."

"You got my number," Macklin said, forcing a smile to his face to hide the despair he feared would creep onto it if he didn't. There would be no more early morning jogs together. Jessica Mordente would see to that tomorrow.

Parks walked toward the oil magnate, and a flash from a camera caught Macklin in its glare and temporarily blinded him. The burning light, though, illuminated something in Macklin's mind that he had overlooked.

He had just ruined Cecil Parks's career.

A shiver coursed through Macklin's body as he realized the implications of his presence in the ballroom. He had been seen with Parks in a friendly embrace, perhaps even photographed together. When the news broke that Macklin was Mr. Jury, the ensuing scandal would now destroy Parks too.

Macklin glanced at Shaw, Sunshine, and Jeffries, then at Parks chatting with the fleshy Arab. All he wanted to do now was go, escape into the night until this nightmare was over. Without bothering to stop by Shaw and Jeffries's table, he turned and left.

CHAPTER SIX

Sunday, 9:47 P.M.

Bruce Springsteen was singing about Cadillac Ranch on the tape deck as Macklin steered the Batmobile off the southbound Harbor Freeway and into the turbulent neighborhood where his father, an LAPD beat cop, was ambushed and set aflame by a street gang.

The urban middle-class neighborhoods where Macklin spent his life were always changing, forever young. The people who lived there wore their neighborhoods like bright white starched dress shirts. Occasionally the shirts got stained, but they could always be washed clean.

These streets here were different. People here wore their neighborhoods like dirty work shirts. Decay encircled the buildings like vines.

Macklin's Cadillac glided almost invisibly down the gray streets, a black breeze moving silently in the dark night. He had driven here almost unconsciously and didn't know where he was going until now. His eyes traced the contours of the gray buildings, read the spray-paint scribbles on the walls, looked into the angry and weary faces, and he wondered how a world so far outside his own could affect his life so much.

In Macklin's middle-class world, this neighborhood could be avoided for a lifetime. It was severed from everyday experience and existed only in the abstract. Never did the two worlds have to meet.

Not true for Brett Macklin. This neighborhood had seeped through some crack in the barrier and was now spilling like a waterfall into his life. It had suddenly swept him up and now he couldn't escape its treacherous currents.

Macklin turned the car around a corner. He saw the hamburger-shaped restaurant down the block and the revolving, blinking sign that read BURGER BOB's atop the sesame-seed-bun roof.

The river that had swept Macklin up over a year ago was surging forward and carrying him over a precipice.

Burger Bob, his broad belly wrapped in an apron and his balding head capped with a cook's cauliflower top hat, looked like the Pillsbury Dough Boy smoking a cigar.

With the cigar stub clenched in the corner of his mouth, Burger Bob scrawled down the order the two jittery black guys on the other side of the counter had given him.

"What'll ya have on your burgers?" he asked, looking up from his note pad and down the barrel of a Saturday night special. He felt his heart drop like a boulder into his foot.

"All the cash in the register," grinned the black guy in the oil-stained undershirt, waving his gun toward the register for emphasis. "And hold the mayo."

The black guy next to him screeched with laughter, his mouth open wide as if he expected to catch a baseball with it. His missing lower front teeth suggested he might have tried once. Burger Bob didn't notice. Burger Bob's eyes were on the gun shaking in Big Mouth's hand.

There was no one else in the restaurant. The last time Burger Bob was held up, some short guy eating a cheeseburger and fries tried to be a hero and ended up swallowing two bullets for dessert. The *Los Angeles Times* spread the news over the top of the Metro section and business slowed for three months.

"Move, fatso, or your brains are gonna be sizzling all over that grill behind you," the guy spoke again.

Burger Bob hesitated, fear cementing him to the floor. Suddenly the gun bucked in Big Mouth's hand, shaking the restaurant with a tremendous roar. Burger Bob screamed and jumped two feet back, his buttocks slamming into the grill. His hat fell onto the floor. The bullet had scorched a hole through the center of the hat.

"Bufus don't tell a man nothin' twice, asshole," Big Mouth said. "You want to inhale the next bullet? Get us the cash."

"To go," Bufus grinned.

Burger Bob saw a flash of red behind Big Mouth and everything became a slow-motion nightmare. A blast thundered in Burger Bob's ear and then Big Mouth was flying over the counter, his arms reaching out for him, his eyes wide and white. Burger Bob flung himself sideways, felt Big Mouth sail past him, and then heard the dull thud as the black man collided with the wall and dropped onto the grill.

As Burger Bob rose, the dream state dissipated and the world returned to normal speed. Big Mouth lay crumpled facedown on the grill, tiny curls of smoke rising from his body as he sizzled like raw hamburger in his own blood. The gun slipped from Big Mouth's lifeless fingers and clattered to the floor.

"You're a real comic genius, nigger."

Burger Bob turned to see who had spoken and saw a man in a red jumpsuit standing behind Bufus, who stood still as a statue, his eyes to the floor.

"Drop the gun," the stranger said, his .357 Magnum held steady in his right hand.

Bufus dropped his Saturday night special, which landed heavily on his foot. He forced back an agonized wail, his face wrinkling in pain.

The stranger laughed with sputtering dry heaves that sounded like he was gagging. Bufus wasn't laughing. He was wincing. "That was funny," the stranger said. "A joker like you should appreciate that." He walked around to face Bufus and grinned. "We're gonna have some more laughs, aren't we, Bufus?"

The stranger jammed his gun into Bufus's groin. Bufus doubled over, a guttural cry of pain escaping from his throat. The stranger pushed the gun into his testicles. "Move back and lie down on the table," the stranger said, forcing Bufus back by digging his gun into him.

Bufus hit the table with his buttocks and then lay flat on his back atop it, knocking a napkin container and a salt shaker to the floor.

"Close your eyes and open your mouth wide," the stranger hissed, his gun still pressed into Bufus's groin. "You so much as breathe funny and I'll decorate the wall with your balls."

The stranger turned his head toward Burger Bob. "Bring me a ladle of french-fry oil."

"Please, mister—" Bufus pleaded. The stranger jabbed his gun into his testicles, choking back Bufus's words.

"Keep quiet, nigger."

Burger Bob, a ladle of boiling oil in one hand and Big Mouth's gun held unsteadily in the other, shuffled nervously up to the stranger.

"Thanks, friend," the stranger said, taking the ladle from Burger Bob and flashing an amiable smile. "Now please step aside where it's safe."

The stranger looked down at Bufus, who jerked as though an electrical current were running through him. He tipped the ladle over Bufus's gaping mouth. "Eat hot death, nigger."

"Hold it!"

A drop of boiling grease dropped onto Bufus's cheek as the stranger turned to face the voice. A tuxedo-clad Brett Macklin stood poised in the doorway, his .357 Magnum trained on the man in red. Heavy, sludge-brown smoke billowed out of the kitchen, blanketing the room in the thick odor of charred meat.

To Burger Bob, it was beginning to look like a grisly costume party.

The stranger's lips curled into a smile. "Hey, it's okay, I'm Mr. Jury." He kept the tipped ladle poised over Bufus's mouth.

Bufus whimpered, tears streaming from his closed eyes and trickling onto the table.

"No, it's not okay," Macklin hissed, stepping into the center of the dining room. "And you're not Mr. Jury."

He could see the stranger's face tighten and his makeup-shrouded eyes narrow on Macklin's .357 Magnum. Macklin saw the stranger's eyebrows arch in realization and noticed him nodding his head slightly.

Then Macklin sensed a motion behind him. Before he could turn, an explosion of pain burst in his head and he felt himself tumbling forward into a swirling, murky gray cloud.

His eyes were open, but it was like looking at the world through wax paper. Macklin was aware of Burger Bob standing over him, holding Big Mouth's gun by the barrel. Burger Bob had smacked him a good one with the butt of the gun.

Macklin could barely make out the outline of the phony Mr. Jury as he poured the hot oil into Bufus's mouth. The black man thrashed wildly. His back slapped against the table, becoming an incessant, agonizing beat that echoed in Macklin's head. Macklin willed his limbs to move, but they wouldn't obey him. He felt as though he was paralyzed from the neck down.

"Thanks, Mr. Jury," he heard Burger Bob say. "Those black animals have been terrorizing me for years."

A man's shadow fell over Macklin and, through the foggy haze of semiconsciousness, he saw the phony Mr. Jury point his gun at him.

"It's all right," the gunman said. "Us white people have to stick together. It's the White Wash way."

"It's the American way," Burger Bob replied.

Inky blackness dropped like a curtain over Macklin's eyes, and he felt himself plunging into a bottomless abyss. He saw some light ahead and suddenly he felt himself fall through the ice of a frozen lake, the chilly water enveloping him.

Macklin coughed and his eyes sputtered open. Burger Bob stood over him, holding a pitcher of water. He splashed some more water on Macklin, who sputtered and held his hands up in surrender.

Burger Bob held a hand out to Macklin. He grabbed Burger Bob's outstretched hand and pulled himself up to a standing position. The restaurant felt like a boat on stormy seas. The floor seemed to roll on unseen swells.

"Get out of here, you dumb fuck." Burger Bob handed Macklin his .357 Magnum and jerked his head toward the door. Macklin massaged the back of his head and glanced at Bufus. The black man's limp arms and legs dangled off the edges of the table like the corners of a large, bunched-up tablecloth. Steam escaped from his wide mouth and clouded his open, dead eyes.

"Get out of here," Burger Bob insisted, poking Macklin in the stomach with the barrel of Big Mouth's Saturday night special. Macklin acquiesced, his stomach churning with nausea. He turned slowly and dragged himself weakly to the door.

"What the hell were you doing, anyway?" Burger Bob shouted at him. "Mr. Jury is a godsend!"

Midnight.

"It was that gun, and the way he said it." The caller's panicky voice was shrill and irritating. "We've got trouble."

Anton Damon sighed and absently arranged the peanuts on the table in front of him into two large W's. "You think he may have been the real Mr. Jury?"

"Yeah," the caller replied. "I mean, you shoulda heard the way he said, 'You're not Mr. Jury.' He knew, man. He really *knew.*"

"That does complicate things," Damon said. "It means Mr. Jury was never killed. It means that people, perhaps even the police, have mounted an organized effort to cover for him and we have endangered that."

"So what do we do?"

"Nothing," Damon said flatly. "Absolutely nothing. We sit tight for now and see what happens. Mr. Jury's unexpected resurrection may help our cause."

"And if it doesn't, what then?"

"We find him and kill him."

CHAPTER SEVEN

Monday, May 21, 8:30 A.M.

B rett Macklin was awake, but he didn't want to move. This, he knew, was his day of reckoning. He wanted to lie in bed forever.

The sheets were twisted into heavy ropes around his perspiring, naked body. The side of his head was nuzzled comfortably in a warm pocket formed by his pillow. He could see sunlight spilling in through the window curtains, which were billowed by gentle puffs of lukewarm morning air.

Every time he began to move, someone pounded a wooden stake into his skull. Macklin had Burger Bob to thank for that. The pain was a tangible reminder of his dismal failure during the confrontation with the phony Mr. Jury.

Macklin cursed himself for not killing the sadistic madman when he had the chance. How could he have let the impostor get away?

After Macklin left the restaurant, he called Shaw to warn him about the two murders and learned from Shaw about the death of the black prostitute. The phony Mr. Jury, Macklin realized, was even sicker than he had imagined.

But now there was nothing Macklin could do about that. Tomorrow he would be in jail, his life destroyed. Macklin rolled over onto his back and took a deep breath. The circulation returned to his paralyzed arms and legs, making them feel like sacks filled with scurrying ants. As the paralysis waned, Macklin untangled himself from the sheets and sat up.

His sinuses were clogged up and his eyes burned. He combed a hand through his slumber-matted brown hair, coughed, and stood up. The wooden stake drove deeper into his skull, and he could feel his heart pulsing behind his forehead.

Macklin stepped into a pair of jogging shorts which had been lying on the floor and pulled them up around his waist before he left the bedroom. Holding the handrail, Macklin trudged down the stairs to the front door, opened it, and brought in the morning *Los Angeles Times*. This, he assumed, was his last morning of freedom, and he wanted to spend it in the routine, pleasant way he always had.

He flipped through the sections of the paper as he shuffled into the kitchen. Jessica Mordente's interview with Anton Damon covered the front of the Metro section. Macklin dumped the paper onto his butcher block table, opened the refrigerator, and pulled out a carton of orange juice and half a cantaloupe. He took a spoon out of a drawer and brought his breakfast to the table.

Taking a big gulp of juice from the carton, he began reading Mordente's story. He hadn't read her work before and he thought he might as well see if he was going to be exposed by a good writer. Macklin found himself paying less and less attention to the writing and more and more to Damon himself. Damon's racist views hadn't changed, though his low-key delivery was a sharp contrast to his outspoken preprison days. Macklin remembered when Damon came to UCLA and caused a riot by rallying the students to urinate on the administration building to protest the increased minority enrollment.

Damon was no longer the fascist firebrand. Macklin thought Damon came off now like a right wing, conservative politician. Although Damon danced around the issue of whether or not he was still the leader of the White Wash, it seemed clear he was working hard to give the group some mainstream legitimacy.

It was like the Hell's Angels trying to convince people they were really the Mickey Mouse Club, Macklin thought.

He found the new, politically aware Damon a far greater threat than the revolutionary youth he once was. Damon, according to the article, had even hired a media consultant to further hone his mainstream image.

Macklin turned the page and felt anxiety grab his guts and squeeze them. MR. JURY KILLS TWO BLACKS IN SADISTIC BLOOD-BATH, the headline screamed, followed by a subhead reading: Local Leaders Fear Race War Brewing.

His morning routine was shattered. Reality leaped from the page and slapped him in the face. Macklin brought the paper close to his face with trembling hands and scanned the story.

> "He said he would protect innocent people from black lawlessness," said Robert Roberts, owner and operator of Burger Bob's restaurant. "He said us white people have to stick together." ...

Burger Bob made no mention of Macklin. Several random quotes from people on the street praised the phony Mr. Jury and supported the impostor's remarks about blacks. Community leaders, the article said, feared that Mr. Jury's racist views, because of the vigilante's popular appeal and media attention, could heighten racial tension and spark a race war.

Macklin reread Burger Bob's quote again and again. There was something missing.

"He said us white people have to stick together."

He lowered the paper, feeling a hot flush sweep over his body. A raspy voice whispered to Macklin through hazy memories.

"It's all right, us white people have to stick together. It's the White Wash way."

The phony Mr. Jury, Macklin suddenly realized, worked for Anton Damon. Macklin grimaced. It was diabolical but brilliant.

Damon didn't really have to gain public trust to get people to listen to his racist doctrine. He'd let Mr. Jury, someone the public already supported, someone the public saw as a hero, do it for him. The phony Mr. Jury, Macklin realized, was a White Wash power play paving the way for the emergence of Anton Damon as a right-wing political force.

He bolted from his seat, grabbed the phone receiver off the wall, and punched out Jessica Mordente's home phone number with his index finger. He had to make her understand.

The phone rang twice.

"Hello?" Mordente answered.

Macklin's hand tightened on the receiver. "This is Brett Macklin. I made you a promise and I'm ready to honor it."

"What you made was a stalling tactic so you could indulge yourself in one last kill," Mordente yelled, her voice quivering as she held back her tears of fury.

"Listen to me, I—"

"People end up dying when I listen to you," she broke in. "You're inhuman, Macklin, a monster."

"It's Anton Damon, Jessie. He's the one behind all this. The phony Mr. Jury is Damon's stooge," Macklin said. "Don't you see? Mr. Jury is already part of the public's collective consciousness as a good guy, a positive force. Damon is using that to propagate his racist drivel. He's going to get a lot of people killed."

"Fuck off, Macklin. Save it for your trial," Mordente barked.

Macklin exhaled slowly. She wasn't going to listen. There was no use trying to convince her. Face it, Macklin told himself, it's over for you. There's nothing you can say to her to stop it. "Okay, Jessie, how do you want to play this? I can come over to your place. I could be there in Brentwood in fifteen minutes."

"No way, Macklin. You're not getting me alone," she said. "Meet me downtown at the *Times* office. We can talk in the newsroom. Then I'm calling the cops." She hung up.

Macklin rapped the receiver against the wall like a hammer. There was nothing he could do. It was over. He felt none of the sadness he had felt before, only anger. He would be behind bars, and his family shamed, all for nothing. The phony Mr. Jury's murders would be attributed to him and eclipse any arguments he might make to justify his vigilante work. Worst of all, Damon's psychopath would still be free.

Taking a deep breath, Macklin called Los Angeles Mayor Jed Stocker on his private line at his office. Stocker was always in the office by 8:00 A.M., thumbing through morning papers and watching "Good Morning America."

"I thought I should warn you," Macklin said. "A reporter is going to—"

"Forget it, Macklin," Stocker interrupted. "Mordente won't write her story."

Macklin was stunned. "What?"

"I put a couple of voice-activated bugs in your house a few months ago," Stocker said. "Unfortunately, I didn't get around to listening to the tapes from Friday until last night."

"You rotten son of a bitch," Macklin hissed. "Who the hell do you think you are?"

"You can shove your fucking indignation up your goddamn ass, Macklin. I'm saving us all," Stocker shot back. "My people are on their way to take care of Mordente right now."

A chill of fear brought goose bumps to Macklin's skin. "You're going to have her killed," Macklin stated.

"Yeah, that's right, Macklin," Stocker said cockily. "That's the way it has to be."

"My God, Stocker, are you crazy? You can't just go out and kill someone!" Macklin shouted into the phone.

Stocker chuckled derisively. "What the hell do you think *you've* been doing, Macklin? You don't think what you do is killing?"

"That's different, Stocker. Those people were murderers," Macklin barked. "Mordente committed no crime. She's the public we're supposed to be protecting!"

"Damn it, wake up, Macklin! Mordente will ruin us all. The scandal she'll create will plunge this city into anarchy," Stocker said. "She must be sacrificed for the greater good of this city."

"No," Macklin insisted. "You've got to stop it."

"It's too late," Stocker said. The line went dead.

9:15 A.M.

"Could I please see your license and registration?" asked the police officer. The traffic on the Santa Monica Freeway surging eastward was a blur behind him.

Jessica Mordente frowned, stretched across the car to her glove compartment, and saw that another police officer was standing on the passenger side. *The fuckers. Of all the goddamn mornings to get on my case....* She rummaged around the cassette tapes, maps, and notebooks for her registration papers and snuck a glance up at the cop. He looked like a clone of the guy on the driver's side. Both hid their eyes behind reflective sunglasses and wore crisp, pressed blue uniforms.

Fascist assholes, Mordente thought. If I don't hurry, Macklin is going to get to the *Times* before I do.

Mordente sat up in her seat and handed her registration to the cop on the driver's side and then pulled her tattered driver's license from her purse and gave that to him too. He gave both papers a cursory glance.

"Please step out of the car, Ms. Mordente."

Mordente narrowed her eyes, perplexed. "Why? What have I done wrong?"

"Just step out, please."

Mordente heard the officer on the passenger side unclip the strap over his gun. Her heart fluttered. *What is going on here?*

She opened the door and stepped out. She felt the officer's strong hand grasp her arm and guide her toward his black-and-white four-door Plymouth. As he led her to the rear of the police car, she read the emblem on the door: TO PROTECT AND TO SERVE.

"Hey, you guys aren't the highway patrol," Mordente said. "You're LAPD. What are you doing on the freeway giving traffic citations?"

He reached around her and opened the back-seat door. "Get in, Ms. Mordente."

"You haven't told me what I've done wrong," she protested. "Am I under arrest or what?" She looked at his name tag. It read: Victor Deese. "You had better start doing some talking, Officer Deese."

Deese shared a glance across the roof of the police car with his partner. Without warning, he twisted Mordente's arm painfully behind her back and rammed her face forward against the open door. Before she had a chance to struggle, she felt the cold steel of a handcuff close tightly around her wrist. Deese yanked back her other arm and cuffed it.

Mordente spun around, enraged, her arms restrained behind her back. "What kind of bullshit is this? If you two think you can get away with this harassment, you're wrong."

"Get in the car before I push you in," Deese said between clenched teeth.

He meant it, she knew, and that scared her. Mordente reluctantly ducked into the back seat. Deese slammed the door closed and then slipped in behind the steering wheel. His partner sat down beside him. They were separated from Mordente by steel grillwork. Deese eased the car into the flow of traffic. The cop on the passenger side leaned against the door and looked at her. His name was Ron Laird.

"This isn't an arrest, is it?" Mordente asked coolly.

Laird grinned and shook his head from side to side.

"What is it?" she asked.

"A murder," Laird replied.

CHAPTER EIGHT

Monday, May 21, 9:22 A.M.

This time he wore a white cotton jumpsuit that read MARINA DEL REY TOWERS in curly script over his breast pocket. A pair of dark black sunglasses shrouded his eyes and accentuated the paleness of his face. He stood in the center of the yellow-painted, black-scuffed service elevator as it groaned upward toward drug peddler Aaron Tate's penthouse. No wood grain and Muzak for the hired help, nosiree.

In his left hand, he held a stack of neatly folded clothes chest high in front of him to hide the silenced .357 Magnum. It was still hot from the slugs it spit into the nigger laundryman in the basement. He had made him strip so the jumpsuit wouldn't get dirty and then shot off his balls.

The elevator jolted to a stop and the doors squealed rustily as they slid open, revealing a floor covered in white wood planks to resemble a patio of a country home.

He stepped out. The doors closed behind him and he noticed a second elevator to the right of the service one. He faced forward again. The double doors to Tate's penthouse looked like the front door to a home, complete with ornate brass door knocker, lighted doorbell, and patio doormat. Potted plants flanked either side of the door and a planter box filled with bright flowers rested below the draped bay window to the left of the door.

The nigger drug peddler had certainly made some money. But he wasn't impressed. He had seen a lot of cash thrown around in his life. He pressed his finger against the doorbell. He heard a muted chime from somewhere beyond the door. A dark form passed behind the drapes, and he heard heavy footsteps approach the door.

The door swung open and he saw a tall, bald, cold-eyed black man wearing black satin sweats and a white tank top that was about to tear against the strain of his chest.

"I've got something for you."

"I'll take it," the black man said tonelessly.

The Magnum popped once and the black man stumbled back, his eyes wide, as if he had just swallowed something down his windpipe. Red burst across his white tank top. The black man dropped into a sitting position on the white shag carpet, wavered for a moment, then toppled flat on his back with a thud.

The killer dropped the laundry and closed the door behind him softly. Behind the black's body was a white Steinway piano in front of a picture window that offered a breathtaking view of the frothy Pacific swells. All of Tate's furniture was white. All the pictures were framed in white.

White as the coke Tate sells, he thought. White as the man who's gonna kill him.

He moved toward the hallway to his left.

"Hey," someone said behind him.

The killer whirled, squeezing off two shots into the bathrobe-clad woman who emerged from the kitchen. The first bullet slammed into her shoulder and spun her around. The second burst went through her chest and splattered the wall with her heart.

He turned back to the hallway. Ahead of him was the door leading to the helipad stairwell. To his right was Tate's office door. He pushed it open. A long, uncluttered mahogany desk and another picture window faced him, and the walls were lined with bookcases.

Tate was to his left, riding his white exercycle, his eyes staring out the window at imaginary bike trails. He was trying to work off the ten-pound roll around his middle that poked out underneath his white satin jogging jacket and hung over the waist of his matching pants. His jacket was unzipped to his midsection, exposing a damp, rounded chest decorated with seven gold chains.

"Who the fuck are you?" Tate huffed, trying to hide his surprise with anger.

"Mr. Jury."

Tate noticed the silenced Magnum for the first time and froze on his exercycle. "What have you come to take, huh? Money? Drugs? What?"

He grinned. "Your life, nigger."

9:30 A.M.

The torrent of cars on the Santa Monica Freeway below Macklin's helicopter flowed toward the cluster of skyscrapers mired in the greenish haze to the east. To him, the downtown buildings looked like a tangle of tall weeds in a muddy landscape.

"Mordente has already left her place," Shaw's voice crackled from the headset speakers. "She must be on the road."

Ahead, Macklin could see the cars slowing and blurring into a solid black line of stalled traffic beginning at the distant Crenshaw exit. Traffic inched eastward at a crawl.

"Were you able to find out what squad car Stocker's monkeys are driving?" Macklin heard his own amplified voice echoing in his ears.

"Yeah," Shaw replied. "Deese and Laird are in car fifty-four."

"All right, where are you now?"

"I'm making the transition from the southbound Four oh five to the eastbound Santa Monica Freeway."

"Ten-four, over and out." Macklin heard the whisper of static signaling the end of the transmission.

After discovering Stocker's plans, Macklin called Shaw, gave him a quick explanation, and sent him to the reporter's house. Then, wearing only his jogging shorts and sneakers, Macklin hurried to the Santa Monica airport, slipped a Kevlar vest over his naked torso, grabbed an Ingram and a handful of clips, and took to the skies to search for Mordente.

The helicopter rumbled across the sky. Macklin peered down at the freeway, searching for the white top with the black number 54 painted on it. On the shoulder he saw a parked sports car. He brought the helicopter down and made a low pass over it.

He saw a red Mazda RX-7. Grimacing, Macklin circled above Mordente's car. "Ronny, I've found her car. It's been abandoned about a mile west of the Robertson Boulevard exit. I'm going to continue east, searching the freeway."

"Roger," Shaw responded. "I can see you ahead."

Macklin made one final pass over Mordente's car and saw Shaw's beige Ford sedan roaring down the shoulder, a red light flashing on top. He turned the helicopter away and veered into a parallel course following the freeway. From his vantage point, the city looked like a collection of cardboard buildings and toy cars laid out on a child's dirty bedroom floor.

"I'm coming up behind the car now," Shaw said. "It looks empty."

Scanning the freeway ahead of him, Macklin spotted a black-and-white patrol car shooting free of the congested traffic and gliding down the La Cienega Boulevard exit.

The helicopter bore down in a tight, right arc and streaked southward over the patrol car. Macklin smiled with grim satisfaction. He found car 54.

"Forget her car," Macklin shouted into the mike. "They're heading south on La Cienega Boulevard."

"Take it easy, Mack," Shaw advised. "Don't spook them. I'll take the Robertson exit and haul my ass to La Cienega."

The long boulevard began as a steep slide off the glittering Sunset Strip into the homosexual colony bisected by Santa Monica Boulevard. Then La Cienega seeped into the city like an infection, decaying the area around as it ate its way through to LAX. It turned the flesh of the city absolutely rancid at the rise to Baldwin Hills.

Macklin watched the patrol car pick up speed as La Cienega widened and became a six-lane quasi-freeway to scale the dreary, sunbaked Baldwin Hills, which looked like a lunar landscape covered with dead dune grass. Hundreds of rusty oil pumps bobbed on the foothills and sucked the land dry for Chevron and Getty. Cyclone fences ringed with barbed wire chopped the hundreds of acres into jagged, puzzle-piece chunks of gangrenous land licked by the asphalt tongue of La Cienega Boulevard.

The patrol car turned right onto Stocker Street and into the secluded wasteland. A swirling cloud of dirt billowed out behind the car as it veered off the road and into the vast oil fields.

The sour odor, a rotten smell reminiscent of natural gas and hot tar, blew through the open front windows and into Jessica Mordente's face. The police car sped over the gravel in a winding, upward trail between rusted oil pumps, piles of trash, and corroded piping.

Her head throbbed from the heat, the smell, and the fear. Deese and Laird had been silent since the freeway, though Laird kept looking back at her with a sickly smile on his face. That left her to her thoughts, none of which were very uplifting. She had always thought the police and Macklin were tied together somehow. She never thought they'd do his killing for him.

The car stopped beside a lone oil pump on a tall slope. It's rhythmic, screeching grind was eerily reminiscent of a heartbeat, as if the land were alive. A torn and soiled mattress, its stuffing spilling out, was crumpled against the pump in a patch of dead weeds littered with crinkled beer cans, Burger King bags, and an empty Trojan condom pack. Mordente peered out the window at the surrounding area. The slope was sheltered by a circle of foothills covered with nodding oil pumps.

They were utterly alone.

Deese wearily pushed open his door and stepped out. "Yeah, this will do just fine."

He yanked open the back door, grabbed Mordente around the neck with his left hand, and pulled her toward the door. "Get out, you damn cunt."

Mordente began to get out of the car, met Deese's eyes, then rammed her knee into his groin with every ounce of strength she could muster.

Deese grunted and doubled over. Mordente pushed past him and dived over the edge of the slope, tumbling head over heels onto the loose rocks and dirt. She rolled uncontrollably down the steep face, her hands cuffed behind her back, her eyes closed tight.

Mordente could feel the gravel tearing at her skin and could hear the explosive crack of gunfire above her. Finally, when it seemed like her tumbling would never end, she crashed through a tangle of barbed brush. She lay there dazed on her back for a moment, the world spinning. When the sense of motion subsided, she rolled over on her left and saw Deese and Laird standing on the crest, firing their guns at her. Slugs chewed into the loose dirt around the brush.

Then Deese held his gun up in the air and, half sliding and half running, charged sideways down the hill toward her. Mordente looked to her right and saw only the rise of another foothill. The face of the slope was steep and afforded no cover. If she tried to scale it, they could pick her off with ease.

A current of gravel, kicked out from under Deese's feet, spilled against Mordente. She whipped her head around and saw that he was only twenty yards away, a victorious grin on his face. She heard a chopping sound echoing between the hills and saw Deese's smile wane.

Suddenly a helicopter burst over the crest behind Deese. Laird whirled around. The landing skid smashed through his face and sent his body toppling down the slope. Deese forgot about Mordente and scrambled toward the brush. The helicopter streaked down the hillside and closed in on him like a hawk.

He dived into the brush, rolled, and came up in a crouch, firing two shots at the helicopter, which roared over him, banked, and climbed the face of the hill to Mordente's right. It stopped, hovering high in the air, its rotors thwacking, and turned around in place to face Deese.

"Drop your gun and raise your hands," a voice boomed from the helicopter.

Mordente stared incredulously at the helicopter through the tangle of dry foliage. *Macklin?* Her confusion was now as strong as her fear.

Mordente sensed a motion to her left and turned just as Laird's headless, blood-splattered body rolled into the brush and crashed into her. Stark terror grabbed her and she let out a piercing scream that momentarily distracted Deese. He suddenly remembered his prey and pivoted toward her, aiming his gun at her.

She saw Deese shudder, a splash of red blossoming on his chest. His gun arm faltered. He raised it again and his body jerked, a tuft of hair flying off his head like a golfer's divot. Deese, his face blank, slumped forward as if in prayer.

Shifting her gaze from Deese's crumpled body to the helicopter, she saw the muzzle of a silenced Ingram poking out the window. Macklin retracted the Ingram and brought the helicopter down, chopping up the air and whipping up the loose dirt in a giant brown cloud. Mordente pushed Laird's body away and crawled out of the brush.

She felt two strong hands grab her by the shoulders and pull her up. When she looked up, she saw the concerned expression on Sergeant Ronald Shaw's familiar face.

"Everything's all right now, Ms. Mordente," he said, turning her around and unlocking her handcuffs with Deese's keys. He jerked his head toward the clearing between the two foothills. "Let's get in the copter."

She glanced back at the chopper apprehensively. Brett Macklin sat at the controls, his face rigid with grim resolve.

"C'mon," Shaw urged.

Mordente, not knowing what else to do, ran in a crouch alongside Shaw to the helicopter. Shaw opened the back door and she climbed in. Macklin lifted the helicopter into the air as soon as Shaw was inside. Shaw and Mordente slipped their headsets on simultaneously.

"Mack," Shaw said sternly, "get us over to Marina del Rey Towers as fast as you can."

"This stunt doesn't change a thing, Macklin," Mordente broke in.

"Jessie," Macklin said calmly, "I just saved your life. Doesn't that tell you anything?"

"Yeah, it tells me you remembered at the last minute that if I die that story is published anyway," she shouted, residual fear cracking her voice. Both Macklin and Shaw winced as her voice boomed in their ears. "What did you think killing me would accomplish, Macklin? And why use two crooked cops?"

Macklin sighed with frustration and decided it was best to ignore her for the moment. "Ronny, why are we going to the Towers?"

"I got a call. There's been a hit on Aaron Tate, the black mobster behind eighty percent of the drug traffic in this city," Shaw said.

"Is he dead?" Mordente asked quickly, suddenly the reporter. Macklin grinned to himself, certain now that she was all right.

Shaw peered out the window at the hint of blue water in the distance. "Not yet."

CHAPTER NINE

Monday, May 21, 10:23 A.M.

Macklin's helicopter streaked over Chace Harbor, where the frothy swells were cluttered with all manner of pleasure craft, and across the rooftops of dozens of stylish condominium and apartment complexes.

Looming up in front of Macklin were the four staple-shaped Marina del Rey towers, facing each other and forming an imposing eighteen-story steel cloverleaf without the rounded edges. A shimmering blue swimming pool and lush green putting green filled the center space between the towers.

"It's the tower on your left," Shaw instructed.

The helicopter veered toward the building and closed on it in a slow, gentle descent. Mordente hastily finished wiping the blood off her arms and face with alcohol-soaked gauze pads from Macklin's first-aid kit.

A pale young police officer who looked like he was just out of high school appeared on the roof as the helicopter touched down. He had a perplexed, lost expression on his face. Macklin pushed open his door and jumped out, faintly aware of how strange he must look in his Kevlar vest and jogging shorts. Why, he wondered, had Shaw insisted they come here?

Shaw and Mordente dashed past him. The reporter shot an icy glare at Macklin and stayed close to Shaw's side. Her hair was mussed, her face was lined with scratches, and her blouse and slacks were specked with dirt and blood. Yet she hardly showed the trauma. Her stance was firm and her face reflected strong anger and determination. Her whole body radiated strength. Macklin regarded her with genuine admiration.

Macklin remained at the helicopter and watched while the officer animatedly explained something to Shaw, who waved Macklin over with his arm.

"C'mon, Mack," Shaw yelled over the sound of the whirring chopper blades. Macklin reluctantly sprinted to the doorway to the stairs leading into the building. Their footsteps clattered down the stairwell to the penthouse.

"Tate was found ten minutes ago by one of his aides," Shaw explained as he turned and started down the second flight of stairs. "The aide called the paramedics and the police. Unfortunately, there's nothing any of us can do."

"What do you mean?" Mordente asked impatiently.

Shaw pushed open the door that led to a hallway carpeted with thick white shag. The walls were covered in dark wood. Two medics paced in the hallway in front of a pair of open double doors and turned abruptly when Shaw, Macklin, and Mordente appeared in the hallway. Behind them in the living room, Macklin could see two bodies crumpled on the floor and splashes of blood on the walls.

A medic shuffled up to Shaw and stammered, "Hey, don't be mad at us. We're just following the law here." He raised his hands defensively in front of his chest and nodded his head toward the door to his right. "Touching that guy could get us killed."

"They don't pay us enough to deal with that shit," the other medic said, dispensing with a defensive posture altogether.

Macklin and Mordente followed Shaw past the medics and right through the double doors. Mordente involuntarily grabbed Macklin's wrist in terrified surprise, and froze in the doorway.

Aaron Tate, clad in a white satin jogging suit, lay on his back atop his long mahogany desk. His arms were slit open lengthwise and bound to his sides by steel wires that wound around his body and joined at a lump of gray clay on his chest.

Blood flowed out of Tate's fleshy arms in thick streams that dripped onto the floor and formed a huge, expanding stain in the white carpet around his desk. His eyes were open wide and he was shivering.

"That lump of clay on his chest is contact explosive," Shaw whispered. Mordente, realizing she was grasping Macklin's arm, jerked her hand away as if electrocuted. "It's a mixture of clay and nitroglycerin. If he moves too much, or if someone tries to remove those wires, he'll blow up."

"He's shaking," Mordente muttered, staring at Tate.

"I think that's the idea," Macklin realized. "It's from the blood loss. He's going into shock."

"The bomb squad probably won't get here in time to dismantle the bomb before he bleeds to death," Shaw said. "That is, if his convulsions don't blow him up first."

"What are we doing here?" Mordente asked.

Shaw didn't answer.

"Stay in the hall and get the medics to stand clear of the room," Shaw told the officer.

"You got it, Sergeant," the officer said, stepping away eagerly.

Shaw glanced nervously at Macklin, then at Tate. The detective motioned Macklin to follow him and then strode confidently into the room. "Tate," he ventured.

Tate looked at Shaw with two horrified eyes. "Please help me, Shaw. I'll do anything," he said in a weak, drowsy voice. "I'll give you names, dates, places. Just get me out of here."

Shaw bit his lower lip nervously and stopped a foot short of the desk. Macklin came up cautiously beside him.

"Who did this to you, Tate?" Shaw asked carefully.

Tate swallowed, his shivering increasing. Macklin glanced back at Mordente and saw that she now stood only a few feet behind them, just clear of the creeping bloodstain.

"Mr. Jury," Tate sputtered.

Shaw sighed, looked back at Mordente and then to Tate again. "This man standing beside me, is he the one who did this to you?"

"No," Tate muttered.

"Are you certain?" Shaw insisted.

"Yes," Tate replied, wincing. "I'm not going to make it, am I, Shaw? Am I?" Macklin watched as a wave of violent muscle contractions crept up Tate's legs.

Macklin tapped Shaw in the side with the back of his hand. Shaw watched, transfixed in grisly fascination, as Tate's body shook.

"C'mon, Ronny, let's go." Macklin grabbed Shaw by the arm and led him away slowly. Mordente had backstepped through the doorway into the hall.

"Where are you going, huh?" Tate yelled. "Help me, damn it, help me!" His stomach rose and fell with his anxious breathing. Convulsions wracked his body. "Don't go!"

Macklin pushed Shaw through the doorway into the hall just as Tate burst apart in a whirlwind of blood and flame. A powerful fist of scorching air punched Macklin in the back and flung him against the wall outside the room. He flew into it like an insect splattering against a car windshield. The air rushed out of his lungs and he slid dizzily to the floor, chunks of spongy flesh, cheesy adipose tissue, and thick droplets of blood raining down on him.

Lying sprawled out and dazed on the floor, the world spinning around him, he was unsure if the blood on him was Tate's or his own.

Mordente, flat on the floor beside Macklin, was the first person to stand. She braced herself on the wall and rose shakily to her feet, nearly stumbling on a mangled exercycle wheel. The windy sound of hungry flames filled her ears. The medics, at the far end of the hallway, were beginning to stand up. She peered around the charred door frame into Tate's office.

The carpet where Tate's desk had been was aflame, tongues of fire snapping at the ceiling and flicking out the shattered window into the blue sky. Torn flaps of flesh were plastered to the blood-smeared and fire-blackened bookcases around the room.

"Give me a hand," Shaw said, his voice distracting her from the carnage.

She turned and saw Shaw wrapping Macklin's right arm around his shoulder. Swallowing back the bile rising in her throat, she grabbed Macklin's other arm and together she and Shaw lifted him to his feet.

"Are you all right?" Shaw asked Macklin, whose head swayed weakly from side to side.

"Yeah," Macklin sputtered. "Give me a second to catch my breath." He stood in front of Tate's doorway and stared into the office decorated in gore. Damon's Mr. Jury had to be stopped.

"Do you think you can fly your copter?" Shaw released Macklin's arm and was glad to see his friend could stand on his own.

"Yeah," Macklin nodded, glancing away from the room and at Mordente. She didn't look like she agreed with his answer. "Help me up the stairs," he told her.

"Hurry up. I want you out of here before this place is crawling with cops asking a lot of questions," Shaw urged them. "I'll touch bases with you later."

Macklin nodded and they struggled to the stairwell, the door closing behind them just as the bomb squad appeared at the opposite end of the hall.

Hot water pounded from the shower massage into the sore muscles between Brett Macklin's shoulder blades. Dried blood washed off his skin and swirled around the drain, reminding him of the murder scene from *Psycho*. A hand suddenly pulled back the shower curtain and Macklin jumped back, nearly losing his balance on the slick enamel of his bathtub.

"Take it easy," Jessica Mordente said softly, lifting her slim, naked leg over the bathtub rim. Macklin closed his eyes, relieved, and exhaled slowly. He had expected Norman Bates to slash him with a knife.

When he opened his eyes, Mordente stood bare in front of him. Water sprayed off his shoulders in a fine mist that coated her breasts with tiny beads. Her eyes met his and he felt her trembling fingers brush his chest.

She had already taken a shower. While she was doing that, Macklin had scoured the house, found all of Stocker's listening devices, dropped them on his garage workbench, and crushed them with his hammer. He was brewing a pot of fresh ground coffee when she came downstairs. When Macklin had left her a few minutes later, she was curled up on the couch in his terry-cloth robe and sipping a cup of hot coffee.

"Being alone downstairs, all I could think about was all the bloodshed." Her voice was raspy and her shaky fingers traced circles around his nipples. "I need to be with someone."

Macklin understood how she felt. He had endured the same empty, floundering sensation when he first began his vigilance. Only, for him there was no one around to turn to. The fear, the disgust, and the uncertainty had just chewed away at him. But he was past that now. Death was no longer a stranger to him.

Her hands slid across his flat stomach and down to his buttocks. She gently kneaded the firm flesh and drew him closer until he could feel her warm breath on his face. He held her by the shoulders and kissed her lips, feeling her pliant body melt against his.

He pulled back and let his hands slip from her shoulders to the smooth swell of her breasts. While kissing her, he lightly stroked her nipples with the palms of his hands. Her excited nipples hardened, poking into his palms. Her head fell back against the tile and her breathing became ragged.

"Suck them, please," she urged him in a dreamy, far-off voice. Macklin lowered his head, tenderly cupping her breasts and flicking his tongue across one of her pointed nipples. Then he encircled it with his lips, sucking and rolling his tongue across the soft aureola. The shower's hard stream massaged his neck, the hot water cascading in sheets down his arched back and soothing his aching muscles.

She moaned, her back pressed to the cold tile, her hands tightening on his shoulders. He placed his right hand between her legs and let his fingers slip deeply into the softness there.

Mordente's legs began to shake and she slid, moaning, down the tile into a sitting position with her knees bent in front of her. The pulsing water drilled the tile above her head. Macklin stood and felt the hot water punching his sore back again and the luscious warmth of Mordente's mouth around his stiffening penis.

She sucked and licked him with abandon, holding his erection with one hand and milking his testicles with the other. Macklin heard himself groaning with pleasure and was aware of his hips instinctively jerking back and forth. The tingling pressure of his excitement was becoming too much.

Macklin, breathing hard, gently pulled himself away from her and unclasped the shower massage from the wall. He adjusted the dial to soft massage, spread her legs, and held the head over her auburn pubic hair. Jets of water splashed between her legs in rhythmic pulses. She writhed, dragging her fingernails across the tile and clenching her teeth.

"Now, Brett, now," she managed to mumble, tossing her head and lifting her hips closer to the shower head. Macklin dropped the shower head, pulled Mordente toward him, and thrust his throbbing penis into her, both of them crying out with ecstasy as he began thrusting.

They were lost in their own passions, and the horrors they had witnessed today no longer existed. Their bodies slapped together, their pleasure-filled, breathy moans resonating off the tile walls and intensifying as their excitement grew unbearable.

The dwindling rays of the afternoon sun melted into the blue-gray shadows of approaching nightfall. Macklin, propped up against the headboard, stared out his bedroom window at the changing contrast of the trees set against the sky. Usually, he didn't notice the subtle transformation of light to dark. Now there was an emptiness about it that chilled him.

Jessica Mordente nuzzled closer to him, shifting her head from his chest to the warm space between his neck and shoulder. He felt her lips lightly caress his neck. He had told her everything, sharing with her every detail of his life since his father's death. Then they made love again with a hypnotic slowness that built to a frenetic climax that left them sweaty and languid in each other's arms.

"Does it scare you?" she whispered. It was the first time she had spoken since Macklin had told his story.

"What?"

"The thin line that separates you from the fake Mr. Jury."

Macklin said nothing.

"You don't think you two are much alike, do you?" she asked softly, her breath warming his neck.

"I don't have as much hate."

"C'mon, Brett, sure you do."

Neither of them said anything for several long moments. Macklin felt warm and snug under the sheets. The sun had disappeared and the bedroom was dark. His skin was sticky with sweat where Mordente was pressed against him. Her body was like a smoldering fire.

"I don't kill because I like it and I don't kill because I disagree with someone's skin color, religious beliefs, or political bent," Macklin said.

"You kill because you think you're right. You kill to protect someone or to uphold the law. But by the very act of killing, you're making a mockery of the law you force others to abide by with their lives," she said. "So far, the people you've killed probably deserved it. But what about tomorrow or the next day, or the day after that?"

Macklin sighed. "I have to have faith in myself. I have to hope that I'll know if I've slipped over the edge into the kind of madness that's driving him. I know, I know. He thinks he's making things right too. But *I am*. That's the difference."

"It's all how you look at it, Brett."

"How do you look at it?"

"I don't know," she replied, her voice shaky.

Macklin squeezed her tightly against him. Her smooth body felt good and solid against him. He found the feel of her body close against his fortifying and comforting.

"I'm sorry, Brett," she whispered. "I came very close to ruining a good man."

"There's nothing for you to apologize for, Jessie. You were doing what you thought was right."

"A part of me knew it couldn't be true," she said. "But I would have destroyed you anyway."

"It's over now." Macklin buried his lips in her hair.

"No, it isn't." She sat up, leaning forward on her elbows, and gazed into Macklin's eyes. "There's still a killer out there. You aren't going to rest until you get him, are you?"

Macklin nodded.

"I want to help you," she said firmly. He knew he couldn't talk her out of it. He wasn't sure he wanted to.

"When's your next interview with Anton Damon?"

"Thursday."

Macklin leaned forward, brushing his lips against hers. "Bring me with you as your photographer."

"Okay," she replied huskily, slipping her hand under the sheets and down his thigh, "on one condition ...."

CHAPTER TEN

Tuesday, May 22, 11:30 A.M.

"There is no tangible connection between me and your vigilante," said Anton Damon, tilting back until his chair tapped the interrogation room wall, "besides a similar view of the world, Sergeant Shaw."

The black detective unbuttoned his collar and loosened his tie. He could feel perspiration rolling down his back. It was 102 degrees outside and, Shaw mused, 125 inside.

"C'mon, Damon, let's cut the shit." Shaw leaned against the wall facing Damon, who sat at the end of the table beside his attorney, Steve Gregson. Shaw figured that Gregson would gladly trade his Century City office and Mercedes convertible for a thatched hut on Malibu beach and surfboard with a cellular phone. Gregson's sandy blond hair, seamless tan, and bright blue eyes made Frankie Avalon tunes ring in Shaw's ears. "The phony Mr. Jury is White Wash, and those illiterate reprobates can't piss unless you help them aim."

"Mr. Damon, being a parolee doesn't mean you've forsaken your constitutional rights," Gregson sneered at Shaw. "You don't have to answer these ridiculous, loaded questions."

Damon shrugged. "Relax, Steve. Let Sergeant Shaw here flex his muscles. It's amusing." The White Wash leader cocked an eyebrow. "What makes you think this isn't the real Mr. Jury?"

"The real Mr. Jury is dead," Shaw replied. "And while he was alive, he didn't hunt down blacks for sport. This man does, and calls it the White Wash way. Your way."

"Shaw, you aren't thinking," Damon said, giving Shaw a reproachful glare and waving a scolding finger at him. "Mr. Jury is a vigilante who protects people from violent crime. I've yet to meet a black who hasn't committed a crime and wasn't a potential killer. It's only natural that blacks dominate the list of criminals Mr. Jury has, uh, restrained."

"You are amazing." Shaw approached Damon, looking down at the White Wash leader with disgust. "You sit there, glib as hell, talking about potential killers as if you're the Pope. You butchered three human beings."

"I wouldn't call them that," Damon smirked.

Shaw whipped Damon across the face with the back of his hand, the slap of flesh cracking like lightning in the tiny room. Gregson bolted out of his seat but was halted by Damon's upraised hand.

Damon, still smirking, a red mark on his cheek where Shaw struck him, stared into the detective's furious eyes. A uniformed police officer yanked open the interrogation room door. Shaw stepped back, combing one hand through his hair and waving the officer away with the other.

"Like I said, Shaw, I've yet to meet a black man who wasn't a criminal," Damon huffed. "I believe he just broke the law, Steve."

Gregson grinned. "Damn right he did, and I'm going to file a formal complaint."

Shaw's back was to them. He couldn't believe he had let Damon get to him. The racist bastard had won this round. Shaw could barely contain the urge to wring Damon's neck until it crunched between his fingers.

"Sergeant Shaw," Gregson chided, "I demand you either charge Mr. Damon or release him immediately."

Shaw turned around slowly, his anger waning into weary frustration. Sometimes the law made him feel as if he were hogtied. "Damon isn't going anywhere. We're keeping him in custody until we can investigate his parole violations."

"What violations?" Gregson yelled.

"Associating with known felons, for starters." Shaw pulled a sheaf of papers folded lengthwise from his inside jacket pocket and dropped them on the table. "All these people are sharing quarters with him at the Threllkiss retreat."

Gregson stacked the scattered papers neatly and placed them into his thin leather briefcase and snapped it shut. "You'll be out of here in twenty-four hours, Mr. Damon. I promise you that."

Damon made a steeple with his fingers and smiled at Shaw. "No problem, Steve, Take your time. I'm in no hurry."

12:45 P.M.

Mayor Jed Stocker rarely left the movie star's house in a good mood. Now in his three-piece suit and carrying his tennis clothes in a duffel bag and his racket under his shoulder, Stocker strode around the ornate marble fountain in front of the manor and walked to his car. The experience of playing tennis with the big-name actor, who had a string of R-rated box-office successes that were critical disasters, always brought some troubling truths home for the Mayor.

For one, the movie star always kicked the shit out of him on the court so Stocker, who thought he was a pretty hot tennis player, left feeling like the beginner he actually was. And while Stocker ran all over the court trying to sustain volleys, the movie star casually bragged about the naked, buxom starlets he got to fuck for the cameras.

What bothered Stocker was that the movie star was actually *paid* to hump beautiful women. So while the movie star talked about lying on top of Catherine, Raquel, Jacqueline, Lynda, Bo, and the rest, Stocker was left to ponder his less-than-scintillating erotic encounters with his wife, Norma, and his occasional furtive meetings with the shoe repair lady with the compact buns.

Whenever Norma uttered her "I'm too bored to fuck" line, it was off to get those suede shoes fixed and his gonads fired up.

And then there was the final, sobering blow that visiting the movie star always dealt him. Stocker got into his Oldsmobile Cutlass Brougham, started the engine, and drove slowly around the fountain and past the movie star's sleek Maserati sports car. As much as Stocker would have liked a finer car, and as much as he could afford one, he knew the public would have a shit fit if he drove something classy. They'd think he was dishonest.

I'm a fucking leader. Why don't they let me live like one? Where are the royal perks? Why can't I drive a nice car? Stocker drove through the gate and thought, like he did every Tuesday, how much he hated playing tennis with the movie star. He let the car coast down the narrow, winding roads that hugged the tall stone walls and tall, densely packed trees that hid the Bel Air mansions from the street.

Stocker was gliding around another curve when suddenly a black car burst into his path from a driveway on the left. He twisted the wheel and slammed the break pedal to the floor. The Olds fishtailed to the left, the tires screeching as they gripped for a hold on the asphalt.

The Olds stopped across the road and rocked from side to side. Before Stocker could get his bearings, the driver's side door was yanked open and he felt rough hands grab him by the shirtfront and pull him out.

Brett Macklin spun Stocker around, slammed him forward against the hood, and yanked the Mayor's right arm up behind his back.

"What the fuck do you think you're doing Macklin?" Stocker yelled, his cheek flat against the car's hood. He could hear the engine humming underneath it.

Macklin pulled up on the arm until Stocker cried out. "We're finished, Stocker. I don't ever want to hear from you again."

"Fuck you, Macklin, you need me."

"You're mistaken," Macklin said softly.

"You're pushing it, Macklin," Stocker blustered, his anger tinged with desperation. "If you value your daughter's future and your health, you'll let go of me right now. Otherwise, I'll expose you and let my men deal with you."

"Deese and Laird are dead." Macklin twisted Stocker's arm up toward his neck until he heard the Mayor's sharp scream of pain and felt the arm tear free of its socket.

"You're on the wrong side now, Stocker. You better stay away from me and watch yourself," Macklin said, leaning close to Stocker's ear, "or Mr. Jury might just come gunning for you."

Macklin walked back to his Cadillac and left Stocker whimpering on the car, the Mayor's arm hanging limply at a grotesque angle behind his back.

11:00 P.M.

"Attorneys for one-time White Wash leader and convicted murderer Anton Damon allege that his detention for parole violations is police harassment. ..."

Macklin sat in the darkness of his living room, his face lit by the glow from the television screen. The silver-haired anchorman, dressed in a red jacket with the station logo on the breast pocket, related Gregson's complaints in a dull, detached monotone and then switched to a taped interview with Gregson on the deck of his Malibu beach house.

"Sergeant Shaw, I should mention, is a black. My client believes that Sergeant Shaw is simply trying to sanction him for his using his right to free speech provided by the Constitution," Gregson said. High afternoon waves crashed against the sand and crawled up the beach behind him. "He didn't bring Mr. Damon in for alleged parole violations or his alleged connection with the Mr. Jury killings. No, he is hassling Mr. Damon because of what Mr. Damon believes."

Macklin sighed and pressed the remote control in his lap to change the channel. Shaw's face, with a microphone thrust in front of it, filled the screen.

"... Mr. Jury is dead. This man's M.O. is entirely different. He is just using the Mr. Jury name as a justification for his actions. He is killing only blacks, and we have reason to believe that he is a member of the White Wash cult, which we all know was founded by Anton Damon."

The camera focused on an Asian woman, the station logo dangling from her necklace into her cleavage. "How do you respond to Damon's claim that this is just thinly disguised police harassment?"

"I don't," Shaw said.

Macklin's phone rang, distracting him from the television. He clicked the set off and lumbered into the kitchen, where the phone rang insistently. Snapping the receiver off the wall with one hand, Macklin opened the refrigerator with the other and looked for something good to eat. "Hello?"

"It's me," Shaw said, his voice dripping with fatigue.

"I just saw you on TV." The refrigerator was full of balls of aluminum foil. He didn't feel like finding out what aged food they contained. Macklin closed the refrigerator and sat down at the kitchen table.

"Yeah, I come off looking like shit," Shaw replied. "Damon will be out tomorrow. Have you talked to Stocker?"

"Yes. I convinced him to stay out of our way."

"How did you manage that?"

"I charmed him with my disarming personality," Macklin said. "So, did you get anything out of Damon?"

"A formal complaint that will probably get me booted from this case," Shaw said.

"What happened?"

"I hit the son of a bitch."

"Hooray, hooray. I don't suppose that loosened him up?"

"I could have shoved bamboo under his fingernails and he still wouldn't have lost that self-satisfied smirk. But I know he's behind it. I can feel it in my gut. It's sitting there rotting like food that won't digest," Shaw said. "This killer could be anyone in his organization. We've asked for a list of White Wash members, but Damon's lawyer naturally will have to hear it from the Supreme Court before they will give it to us."

"What evidence do we have?"

"We've got a lot of nothing. We've got four wildly different descriptions out of those kids. We're trying to meld them, along with your description, into one composite, but who knows if it will even vaguely resemble him. We've also got two strands of hair, which may or may not be from his head, some pubic hair, some of his skin from under the prostitute's fingernails, and a teaspoon of semen. A couple of detectives are running down the plastique, but I don't think it will take us anywhere."

Macklin tapped the table with his fingers. He felt helpless.

"All I can do is put more patrol cars on the street and wait," Shaw said, filling the momentary silence. "Damon and his killer have to make a mistake soon."

"Yeah," Macklin sighed, "but how many people will die first?"

CHAPTER ELEVEN

Wednesday, May 23, 10:15 A.M.

Sergeant Ronald Shaw sat at his desk, his feet up on his desk, and looked across the empty squad room at Wes Craven standing beside the door.

Shaw wondered if anyone ever suggested to Wes Craven that he should rent the space on his forehead for billboards. Craven was stoic as a signpost and Shaw figured the guy must have about two inches of extra skull between his eyes and the errant, dry strands of blazing red hair that lay on his head like dune grass.

Shaw would even be the first to scrawl a message across Craven's face. It would read: SANDBLAST MY MOUTH OUT WITH AJAX. The mint Craven was sucking made the squad room smell like the cube of ice-blue disinfectant found in urinals. Shaw had heard that Craven, who leaned against the wall in his three-piece, Bond Street tailored suit, was obsessed with fresh breath. Craven probably picked up that habit, Shaw assumed, from spending so many hours leaning close to Justin Threllkiss and taking his orders.

The old coot and his decaying dentures must smell like steaming dog shit, Shaw thought, sitting with his crossed legs propped on the edge of his steel, battleship-gray desk.

Craven, of course, was waiting for Anton Damon.

The squad room door beside Craven opened and the man immediately straightened to attention, like a soldier expecting General MacArthur to come bounding in.

Lieutenant Bohan Lieu grinned at Craven as he entered the room. "At ease, Craven."

Craven fell back against the wall and looked straight ahead through the slats of the blinds at the Sumitomo Bank building that bordered Little Tokyo outside.

Lieu was beginning to look like a Hershey's kiss wrapped in a searsucker suit and bow tie, Shaw thought, smiling back at his superior, who had sparkling, playful eyes framed by fleshy eyelids above and tiny bags below. Lieu always had a bag of Sugar Babies on him or stashed in his desk and liked to walk with his hands in his pockets. Shaw respected him and, more importantly, he liked him. There were too many assholes Shaw could respect but not many he could call a friend.

"I hear Mr. Personality has been hanging around here all night," Lieu said, pausing beside Shaw's desk.

"Yep, Threllkiss sent him down here about midnight just in case we decided, as we often do, to release prisoners at two A.M." Shaw swung his feet off his desk and stood up. "Can I steal a cup of coffee from your office?"

"Sure," Lieu said, leading the way to his office, which was a glass-partitioned corner of the squad room. "I wanted to chat with you anyway."

Shaw groaned inside. "Chat" was Lieu's buzzword for trouble. He made a beeline for Lieu's Mr. Coffee, found a Dodgers' mug lying face down on a napkin, took a chance that it was clean, and filled it up. When he turned around, Lieu was sitting behind his immaculately clean desk, unbending a paper clip. Now Shaw was certain he was in trouble.

"Why is it, Ronny, that every time I take a day off to have a cavity filled there's trouble?" Lieu asked rhetorically. Shaw took a seat in front of the desk. "I just found out you took a swing at Damon."

Shaw nodded.

"That's going to cause us both a lot of aggravation."

"I know." Shaw sipped his coffee. "It was a stupid, reflexive thing to do. I can't say I'm sorry I did it, though. The guy is scum."

"Saying the guy is scum isn't going to clear you with the Board," Lieu said. "It was bad timing too, Ronny. It hasn't been that long since the Tomas Cruz thing."

"Are you pulling me off the Mr. Jury case?" Shaw asked.

"Nope, but you won't ever question Damon again and there might be some strict, official repercussions later. There's also the possibility of a lawsuit."

The squad room door opened and Anton Damon, smiling, was escorted in by Steve Gregson and two uniformed officers. Craven popped a fresh mint into his mouth and moved to Damon's side.

"Maybe not," Shaw said, setting his coffee cup down on Lieu's desk. "He's not wearing a neck brace and screaming whiplash."

Shaw and Lieu walked into the squad room.

"Mr. Damon is leaving now, gentlemen," Gregson said, handing Lieu a slip of paper. Damon grinned with satisfaction. "I'll bring you all into court for this outrage."

"If you will come with me, Mr. Damon, I have a limousine waiting at the loading dock," Craven said curtly.

"Thank you," Damon said smugly, shooting a taunting grin at Shaw. "Good-bye, Sergeant. Good luck with your investigation. I'm sure you will reap what you sow."

With that, Damon, Craven, and Gregson left the room. Lieu nodded. "I can see why you socked him."

10:32 P.M.

Anton Damon opened the limousine's refrigerator and made himself a screwdriver while Wes Craven adjusted the color TV and inserted a videotape of last night's newscasts into the portable VCR.

Damon watched the newscasts silently for two or three minutes, sipping his drink, as the limousine hummed east toward the San Bernardino Freeway. Craven sat beside the TV across from Damon, watching the White Wash leader's face for reactions. Craven saw nothing.

"You can turn it off, Wes," Damon said.

Craven pushed off the color TV switch with his thumb.

"What does Mr. Threllkiss think?" Damon asked.

Craven shrugged. "It's publicity," he said. He'd like it if I stayed on with you for a while."

Damon nodded. "I think Sergeant Shaw knows who the real Mr. Jury is."

"Why?"

"A hunch, a look in his eye, the way he talks about him. It also makes good sense. I think the real Mr. Jury is an LAPD puppet."

"What do you have in mind?"

Damon swallowed the remainder of his screwdriver and shook his glass, jingling the ice. "If we get Shaw, we'll get Mr. Jury."

"What if you're wrong? What if Shaw and Mr. Jury aren't connected?"

Damon shrugged, leaning forward to make himself another drink. "So? One less nigger cop."

Thursday, May 24, noon.

The *Los Angeles Times* building looked like the unfortunate victim of an architectural Dr. Frankenstein. The clock-topped cement tower of the once-proud Art Deco building had been grafted on to a block-long cube of brown-tinted glass. The windowy addition was kept nice, shiny, and impenetrable while the chalky remains of its violated host was left to collect grime.

Macklin weaved the car through the First Street traffic, giving the *Times* building a passing glance as it disappeared to his right and the Civic Center blurred to his left. He moved into the left lane. At the stoplight, he looked out the passenger window at Joseph's Men's Wear, "The Store for Mr. Short," and noticed that it was proudly displaying multicolored Sam the Eagle and Olympic Stars-in-Motion neckties in the window.

The tie for the elegant gentleman, Macklin thought. The detectives in Parker Center across the street probably bought them by the dozen.

He turned left on San Pedro, where First Street melted into Little Tokyo, and made an immediate right into a blue-painted steel parking structure. A thin Chicano with a Bela Lugosi hairdo held an MJB can out to Macklin for the twenty-five-cent entrance fee. Macklin dropped the quarter in and then drove the Cadillac up the winding ramp to the top of the structure.

He parked his car on the dividing line between two empty spaces and got out, slinging his friend Mort's camera gear around his shoulder. Mort was in Hawaii and wouldn't miss it. Macklin hurried down the urine-stained stairwell to the street and walked briskly past a gaunt Oriental man selling sushi on Styrofoam plates wrapped in crinkled Saran Wrap.

Macklin sprinted across the street, the cameras bouncing against his side, and was striding up First Street when he saw Jessica Mordente standing on the next corner at the edge of the old *Times* building.

There was a wry smile on her face Macklin couldn't decipher but found attractive anyway. Her hands were thrust deep into the pockets of her pleated silk slacks. Her arms were slightly crooked at the elbows, bunching back the flaps of her matching jacket, revealing a loose-fitting blouse that caught the slight breeze and fluttered. Lois Lane never looked this good.

Macklin dashed across the street on a green light, cutting across oncoming traffic. Horns blared angrily in his wake.

"Do I look like a hotshot news photographer?" Macklin asked.

Mordente frowned, pinning a tattered press ID to his dirty white Paramount Studios sweat shirt. "You look like a tourist, but you'll pass."

She put her hand on the small of his back and led him to her Mazda, double-parked a few feet away. Mordente opened the hatchback and motioned Macklin to take off his camera equipment.

"It's a two-hour drive to Damon's place, so you may as well stow your stuff back here," she said. Macklin dropped the cameras in a clump beside a scruffy shoulder bag covered with out-dated press-pass stickers and pins. He pulled on the strap with one hand. It felt as if the bag were stuffed with bricks.

"What is this thing?" he asked.

"The rest of your cunning disguise. I borrowed it from a photog friend of mine. It's got a bunch of lenses and crap in it. He thinks I'm shooting my sister's wedding," she said, slamming shut the hatch and walking around to the driver's side door. "Get in. There's a six-pack of beer and a couple of BLTs in the icebox behind your seat."

"Great, I'm starving."

Macklin opened the door and dropped himself into the contoured bucket seat. Mordente shifted and the car shot forward with a lurch. She's a little tenser than she looks, Macklin thought. He twisted in his seat, put the icebox on his lap, and opened it.

The fishy stench sprang out into Macklin's face like a jack-in-the-box. "My God, Jessie, how long have you been storing Flipper's carcass in here?"

Mordente shrugged. "Do you want to complain or do you want to eat?"

His growling stomach answered that question. He rum-maged through the icebox while she steered right onto Third Street and onto the southbound Harbor Freeway. He removed two cold Heinekens from amid the ice, took two of the four BLTs out of a zip-lock bag, and helped himself to a bunch of seedless grapes in a plastic bag.

"What can I get you?" he asked.

"Just put a sandwich on my lap," she said. "I'm great at eating and driving. You can wedge the beer between my seat and the gearbox. Gimme a napkin too; they're in the glove compartment."

Macklin tossed a sandwich in her lap, popped open a beer, and crammed it into the tight space beside her seat cushion. The napkins, which had been rolled up and stuffed into the glove box, fluffed out into Macklin's lap when he opened up the compartment. A glare from Mordente stifled his grin and he gave her a napkin.

They ate in silence. Macklin's sandwich tasted like rotten tuna fish and his grapes were so fishy they could have been plump salmon eggs. And even though he spent five minutes wiping the rim of his beer can with a napkin, it still tasted like he was drinking the water out of a goldfish bowl. His hunger overcame his distaste and he ended up eating the other two BLTs and swallowing half of another beer during the ride up to Threllkiss's lakeside retreat.

"Great breakfast, Jessie," he said as they turned off the winding road that rimmed the steep hillside and onto a gravel trail. Ahead, he could see the vague outline of the fence lining Anton Damon's compound and a streak of blue water through the pine trees to his right.

"Let's hope that sadist you saw at Burger Bob's isn't at Damon's place," she said, "or that will have been our last meal."

CHAPTER TWELVE

It smelled like someone's old grandmother lived inside Justin Threllkiss's lakeside home. Outside, there were plenty of Uzis, dark sunglasses, sweat-soaked khaki shirts, mud-caked jeeps, and even a small, dragonflylike helicopter, but not a single grandmother in sight.

Brett Macklin paused in the doorway and let Jessica Mordente enter the house ahead of him. She Lone Ranger, he thought, me Tonto. The guy who opened the door for them had a thick, short neck and a fleshy, insolent face with red circles under his deep-set eyes.

"Howdy, I'm Brett," Macklin said, flashing a toothy grin and thrusting his hand out at Flesh Face. He thought a little Mr. Good Ole Boy might do him some good. "Nice, friendly place you folks got here."

Flesh Face ignored him. Macklin shrugged and followed Mordente into the living room. Anton Damon stood in front of the stone hearth in an Izod polo shirt and jeans, holding a strawberry daiquiri in a frosted glass.

"Welcome, Ms. Mordente, welcome," Damon said, waving his free hand expansively. Two facing couches and a coffee table separated Damon from Macklin and Mordente. Rising from the couch to Macklin's right was a red-haired man with a pale forehead that seemed to glow. "This is my associate, Mr. Craven."

The man with the glossy forehead bobbed his head as his way of saying hello.

"I'd like you to meet my photographer," Mordente said.

Macklin reached around Mordente and pumped Damon's hand enthusiastically. "Brett Macklin's the name. It's a real pleasure, Mr. Damon."

Damon beamed. "Thank you. Where would you like me to stand?"

Macklin dropped the heavy pack on the hardwood floor beside a small stack of freshly cut wood near the hearth. "Right there is fine. You just talk with Ms. Mordente and I'll get you natural. *Posed* is a dirty word with me, Mr. Damon."

"All right," Damon said. "Wes, why don't you bring our guests something cold to drink." He smiled at Mordente and Macklin. "Wouldn't you both like that?"

Mordente opened her mouth to speak when Macklin suddenly cut in. "Yessiree, we certainly would!" Macklin chirped, pushing up his sleeves and crouching beside his pack to rummage through his gear.

Damon nodded at Craven, sending Threllkiss's emissary off to make some fresh daiquiris.

Mordente sat down on the couch that faced the window looking out over the lake. Damon was to her left. She set a tape recorder on the glass coffee table beside a bowl of roasted peanuts.

"Last time we talked about your future. This time I'd like to talk about your past." She scooted into the couch corner and angled herself toward Damon.

While Damon talked, Macklin scrambled around the room taking pictures. He didn't know what the hell he was doing. All his moves were picked up watching reruns of "Lou Grant" and Cheryl Tiegs commercials. But he listened to Damon and kept his eye on the guard movements outside, thereby getting a feel for both Damon and his operation.

Macklin paused every so often to take a drink of his daiquiri. Craven might not ooze charisma but he sure as hell knew how to make a fantastic strawberry daiquiri. It was the first one he'd ever had that didn't taste like a 7-Eleven Slurpee.

"My past is so detached from me. It's like trying to remember the scenes and plot of a movie you saw somewhere once years ago," Damon concluded an hour later. "It's hard for me to connect with the man I used to be. Jesus is standing between him and me, blocking the view."

"So, have you gone back to the dry riverbed where you killed the Kallahans?" Mordente asked. Damon was looking weary; she wasn't. She would probably never run out of questions and had managed to expose some nerves. Macklin, though, had gone through four rolls of film and didn't know whether a single shot had turned out.

"Yeah, yeah, I have," Damon said, holding his glass out to Craven, who had sat across from Mordente through the whole interview and hadn't said a word. But his presence was felt. He reeked of Tidy Bowl. "Can I have another, Wes?"

It was Damon's third. Macklin had helped himself to two. Mordente was still sipping her melted strawberry ice and rum. Craven had nursed a dixie cup of water. Maybe he was watching his weight, Macklin mused. Maybe Craven would splurge and have a saltine for dinner. Craven went past him into the kitchen.

"Anyway, I went out there. I was disappointed," Damon said. "I don't know what I expected to find, a memorial perhaps, an engraved stone or plaque. I thought maybe somebody would have done something to mark the spot. It was an epicenter of a great movement, of a great controversy. Blood was spilled there, lives were changed there, consciousnesses were raised there. Its historic significance has been overlooked." Damon sighed and shrugged. "They're building a new canal or aqueduct or something there."

"Yes, but what did you feel?" Mordente said.

Damon rubbed the side of his nose with his index finger. "I don't know. Sadness. Anger. Wistfulness. Separation. I saw a social movement lingering above the soil like wisps of evaporating dew. I saw an angry young man that I didn't recognize anymore wave a shiny clean ax and grin at me. I saw the Kallahans in the blend of dark shadows cast by the trees."

He shrugged again and Macklin snapped a photo.

"Then I walked away," Damon said, "and bought a double cheeseburger and a chocolate shake at this great Foster's Freeze I know in the Valley. God, it was still as good as I remembered it."

"Okay, let's move on to something else," Mordente said.

"Sure," Damon agreed. Craven returned with new daiquiris for everyone.

"Why don't you move by the window," Macklin suggested out of boredom. Besides, he wanted an excuse to watch the guards along the shore. "We'll change background and lighting a bit, you know? Maybe I'll win a Pulitzer or something, huh?"

Damon obliged, strolling over to the window. Macklin leaned against the back of the couch, twisted the camera lengthwise and held the trigger for a few shots.

"What are your feelings regarding Mr. Jury?" Mordente asked.

"I wondered when you'd get around to that," grinned Damon, walking past Macklin and sitting on the couch beside Mordente. "Now you're going to get brutal."

Mordente smiled.

"I think its unfortunate that people are dying," Damon said. Cagey bastard, Macklin thought.

"Do you also think it's unfortunate that he's getting a lot of publicity and that his beliefs are similar to your own?"

Damon laughed. Craven crinkled his dixie cup and tossed it toward the fireplace. He missed. It bounced onto Macklin's shoe and Macklin threw it in as he got up and sat down next to Craven.

"I don't know what his beliefs are, Ms. Mordente, and I have no feelings on the publicity he's getting. It doesn't concern me," Damon said.

"But he says what he's doing is the White Wash way. Certainly what he does is a reflection on your movement, and you haven't denounced him publicly," Mordente countered.

"For one, he may be a White Wash member but that doesn't mean we endorse him or that he reflects our concerns. I have not made any public statement regarding his actions because I don't want to establish any sort of connection between the two of us, negative or positive. Mr. Jury is Mr. Jury and Anton Damon is Anton Damon. Let's leave it that way."

"The police, by questioning you, have already made the negative connection you speak of."

Damon's smile had slowly disappeared. His lips were tight in grim resolution. "You're right in a way. But I believe the White Wash—Mr. Jury issue was overshadowed by the outrageous, unwarranted behavior of Sergeant Shaw. The issue wasn't Mr. Jury, it was the free expression of ideas. Shaw was acting out a personal vendetta aimed at silencing me. He's a Negro, you know."

Mordente nodded.

"Shaw and the Negro people are afraid of me," Damon said, jabbing himself in the chest with his thumb. "They shouldn't be. I only want to make life better for them. I want them to settle into their proper, God-ordained places. Attaining happiness will be painful for some of them, but happiness always has a cost, doesn't it?"

Macklin took a picture. The tiny click shuddered like a cannon blast in the suddenly silent room.

"That'll be a dandy picture," Macklin grinned.

As the gate swung closed behind them, Macklin reclined in the bucket seat in Mordente's car and exhaled slowly.

"What a frightening bastard," he said.

She nodded. "Do you think he's behind the killer?"

"I'm certain," he replied, closing his eyes.

"What now?"

"You got me. I'm gonna sleep on it."

"Before you start your hibernation, let me ask you one question."

"Go ahead."

"How did the pictures turn out?"

Macklin opened one eye. "Fine. All of 'em are masterpieces. Why?"

"Because my name's going on them, that's why. How do you think I convinced the *Times* not to send a photographer?"

"How will you explain that to Damon?"

"By then, it may not matter."

Damon remained at the couch, staring at the place where Jessica Mordente had sat, thinking how much he would like to fuck her. She looked like a loud one.

Craven appeared from the kitchen. "I just talked with Mr. Threllkiss about your proposal."

"And?"

"He agrees."

"Good," Damon nodded and then yelled, "Dalander!"

Flesh Face lumbered into the room. He was in Laguna shorts with a towel around his neck and he carried a bottle of Coppertone #4 and the latest *Soldier of Fortune* magazine in his hand. He had been on his way out to catch a few rays.

"I want you and our Mr. Jury to grab Sergeant Shaw tonight and bring him here," Damon said. "Use restraint. Don't rough him up any more than you have to."

"Right," Dalander said.

CHAPTER THIRTEEN

Friday, May 25, 3:32 A.M.

"He's with a *white* woman," Dalander whispered, astonished, as he and the killer crept into Shaw's darkened bedroom. Since Dalander was rarely able to convince a woman to voluntarily sleep with him, he didn't see how a black man possibly could. And a *white* woman, at that.

A table fan whirred on the dresser across the bed and sheets were bunched up around the couple's ankles. Shaw and Sunshine wore only bikini underwear and their bodies were slick with sweat.

Sunshine, who slept on the left side of the bed, lay curled against Shaw's back, her arms wrapped around him and her hands resting on his stomach. They looked snug and peaceful.

"Nigger bastard," said the man in the red leather jumpsuit, gliding around Shaw's side of the bed. He grabbed Shaw by the neck with his left hand and yanked him up. Shaw's eyes flashed open and the killer punched him in the face with a right cross, knocking the detective out cold.

Dalander pulled Shaw off the bed by the legs and smiled when his head thudded against the floor. Sunshine rolled over groggily and opened her eyes. Only a terrified gasp escaped her lips before the killer scrambled onto the bed and straddled her half-naked body.

"Keep still. We just saved your life, bitch." He crushed her cheeks in his left hand and coaxed her up into a sitting position.

She could see Shaw's motionless body sprawled on the floor at Dalander's feet. "You should be fucking your own kind. You're lucky we aren't cutting off your tits and turning them into couch cushions."

She closed her eyes, her chest heaving, and tried to choke back her fear.

"That's better," he said. His breath was sour. "Listen. Nigger here has three days to live. Mr. Jury can save his life by showing up, unarmed, at the Hollywood sign at midnight Saturday or Sunday. No show, and the nigger gets chopped up into Puppy Chow. Got it?"

"I don't know who Mr. Jury is," she sputtered, her words muffled by his grip on her cheeks.

He slammed her head back hard against the headboard. "Shut up, bitch. You better meet him then, huh?" Tightening his grip, he nodded her head affirmatively. "Good." With his free hand, he covered her right breast and mashed it flat. "You're a real babe. Maybe you'd like me to come back some night and show you what a real man is like, huh?" Laughing, he forced her to nod her head again. "You'd like to suck my awesome cunt sword, huh?" Again he jerked her head up and down. Releasing her head, he let his hand drop and then drove his fist into her stomach.

Sunshine jerked forward, her mouth gaping open as the air rushed out of her lungs. The killer grinned at her, sat up from the bed, and backhanded her across the face with a loud *thwack!* Sunshine slammed back against the headboard, then fell face forward on the bed.

"Sweet dreams," Dalander said to her, and began dragging Shaw by the legs through the doorway like captured game.

The killer lingered by the bed, staring down at Sunshine. He leaned forward and rolled her over onto her back. Her skin was flushed and she moaned softly, dazed and weak. He knew she couldn't wait. He knew she was ready for him.

He slowly unzipped his jumpsuit. "Stuff the cop into the trunk. I'll be out in a few minutes."

8:47 A.M.

Someone tentatively rapped his fist against Brett Macklin's door. The near-silent thud jostled him a little, but he remained asleep on his back, Jessica Mordente lying on her side to his left.

Again there was a knock at the door, harder this time. Macklin's eyelids fluttered.

Knock, knock, knock.

He licked his dry lips, swallowed, and opened his eyes slowly.

Knock, knock, knock.

Downstairs, someone wanted his attention. Macklin exhaled slowly and slid his legs out from under the covers and set his feet on the floor.

Knock, knock, knock.

Careful not to wake Mordente, Macklin eased the rest of his body out of bed. More knocking. He remembered he hadn't fixed the doorbell yet. A terry-cloth robe lay draped on the towel rack in the bathroom. He put it on, tying it as he hurried down the steps to the door. His eyes stung and his hair felt tangled.

He slipped the bolt and turned the cold doorknob, pulling the door open toward him and taking a step back into the entry hall.

Sunshine stood on his porch in a pink bathrobe and slippers. A bluish welt colored her cheek. Her body seemed lifeless and driven by some supernatural force, like one of the walking dead in a George Romero move.

The shock of seeing her hit him in the chest like a tossed brick.

"Sunshine, what are you doing here?" Macklin asked, taking her cold hand and guiding her inside. He didn't see her car in the street behind her. Could she have walked six blocks like that?

"They've got Ronny," she mumbled.

He closed the door and saw Jessica Mordente standing at the top of the stairs, clutching his maroon wool robe tightly around herself.

"Who, Sunshine? Who's got Ronny?" Macklin asked.

Sunshine sat on the bottom step, her back to Mordente. "You're Mr. Jury, aren't you?"

It was a statement, not a question. Macklin glanced up at Mordente, couldn't read her face, then looked back down at Sunshine. He nodded.

Sunshine sniffled and wiped her nose on her sleeve. "They came in the middle of the night. Two men, one in a red jumpsuit. They took Ronny and said he has three days to live. If you don't give yourself up to them at the Hollywood sign at midnight Saturday or Sunday, they'll kill him."

Macklin's heart thumped furiously like machine-gun fire in his chest. Anger and disgust bubbled acidly in his throat. Mordente eased down the stairs, sat beside Sunshine, and tentatively placed a reassuring arm around her shoulder.

"Did you call the police?" Macklin asked hoarsely.

Sunshine shook her head no. "This is outside the law. It's part of whatever you and Ronny have been doing."

"Are you all right?" He squatted in front of her and wiped a tear from her cheek.

She nodded.

"One of 'em—" she began, but her voice cracked and she started sobbing, her body heaving and tears streaming down her face. Mordente pulled her close.

"Th-The one in red," she choked out in a weak voice, "he raped me."

Macklin stood up slowly, clenching his teeth in grim resolve. Sunshine fell against Mordente and shuddered with deep, woeful sobs. Mordente looked up at him with teary eyes and held Sunshine tightly against her.

"I'll get him back," Macklin said, his hands knotting into fists. "And I'll make those bastards pay."

Noon

Brett Macklin's Cadillac charged down the gravel road toward the White Wash compound gate like a vicious Doberman, its engine growling, its shiny grillwork gleaming like bared, moist fangs.

The guards in the towers that flanked the entranceway began firing at Macklin before his car was even in range. He turned up the stereo. Wagner's "Ride of the Valkyries" boomed from the car's four interior speakers.

The bullets skipped off the Cadillac like hailstones as he closed in on the gate. He wore Levi's, a gray sweat shirt, a Kevlar vest, and .44 Magnum automatic in a shoulder holster. An Ingram lay on the passenger seat.

A guard planted himself in the center of the roadway behind the gate, spread his legs to brace himself, and fired his machine gun at Macklin's approaching car. Macklin pressed the accelerator flat against the floorboard.

The Cadillac burst through the gate, splintering it into a hundred jagged chunks, and plowed into the guard, tossing his body into the air. The body rolled up Macklin's hood, glanced off the windshield, and tumbled into the car's wake.

Macklin leaned forward, squinting through the blood-splashed windshield, and saw a dozen guards spill out of the house and scramble toward him. One of them tossed a grenade. Macklin wrenched the wheel and felt the ground heave under the right side of the car, the explosion spitting dirt into the air. Another grenade erupted in front of him. A wave of dirt splattered against his windshield.

Spinning the car in a doughnut shape, Macklin pushed in the lighter and faced the guards again. The twin .50-caliber machine guns emerged from the front of his car spitting slugs. The guards were cut down in one short, staccato burst. Their bodies were chewed up into fertilizer under the car's tires as Macklin blazed a trail to Damon's front door.

Grabbing the Ingram, Macklin threw open the driver's door and fell out of the car in a crouch, facing the demolished gate and firing.

Three approaching guards did a jerky death dance as a breeze of bullets blew against them. The "Ride of the Valkyries" blared from the car and echoed on the lake. A bullet pinged off the driver's side window behind Macklin's head. He spun, dropped to his side, and rolled, firing at the porch as bullets chipped at the ground where he had been.

Macklin saw Dalander framed in the doorway and squeezed the trigger. A slug carved out Dalander's Adam's apple and painted the front door with it. Flesh Face stiffened and fell forward. Macklin almost yelled, "Timber!" He scrambled across the porch to the door. He kicked it open and flattened his back to the wall. Someone inside sprayed the porch with bullets, pumping several fresh holes into Dalander's corpse. The gunfire stopped and he heard the clattering of footsteps.

He abruptly pivoted low and fired into the doorway. There was no one. He had riddled the wall with bullets. Macklin crept into the entry hall and peered to his left, into the living room where he had photographed Damon yesterday. He cautiously stepped in, his finger tensed on the Ingram's trigger, the .44 Magnum automatic comfortably snug under his left arm.

Macklin sensed a motion to his right and ducked down as a beam of flame streaked across the living room toward his head. It singed his hair as it flashed over his head, bursting through the window behind him and igniting the curtains. Macklin patted down his hair and squatted behind the couch, ready to spring. Anton Damon, he had seen, stood in the kitchen doorway with three tanks of napalm on his back and a flame-throwing nozzle in his hands.

He heard Damon's wild laugh. "You shouldn't have fucked with me, Mr. Jury."

A burst of fire splashed against the couch, setting it aflame. Macklin tossed himself forward into the entry hall. Damon swept the room with flame, trying to torch him.

Macklin turned to face the archway he had just jumped through, heard Damon's approaching footsteps, and showered the fire-engulfed room with bullets. The Ingram jammed—empty. He threw the machine gun aside, whipped out his Magnum, and scrambled through the front door just as Damon appeared in the entry hall, scorching the ground where Macklin had stood.

An arm of crackling flame reached for Macklin, who flung himself off the porch, rolled across the hood of his car, and fell behind it. The fire skipped across the black hood.

Macklin peered over the hood at Damon. Flame lashed out and smashed into the car. Wisps of fire refracted off the armored steel and dissipated. Macklin hunched down, unsure of what to do. A footstep behind Macklin broke his thoughts. He whirled, firing. Two bullets rammed into Macklin's chest, knocking him breathlessly backward. The guard curled forward, the flurry of Macklin's .44 Magnum punches pounding into his stomach.

Macklin braced himself against the Cadillac's fender, tiny sparkles of light dancing in front of his eyes. The vest had stopped the bullets from piercing his skin but hadn't blunted the impact. His lungs were empty and his chest was a plate of pain. He crawled into the car and slammed the door shut.

Damon laughed and sprayed the car with fire. Macklin heard a familiar rumble and saw a helicopter rise over the house. The White Wash copter circled low over the compound, kicking up dirt and whipping black smoke from the burning house, and then hovered in front of the car.

Macklin straightened up in the driver's seat and stared up into Wes Craven's angry eyes. Macklin jerked the gearshift into reverse. The Cadillac wheels tore into the gravel and the car shot backward. Craven veered off and streaked away over the lake. The White Wash leader stood on the edge of the porch, chasing the car with flame. Macklin spun the wheel around and turned the car toward the porch, shifted into drive, and pressed the gas pedal flat.

Damon backstepped and turned, saw the burning doorway behind him and faced the oncoming car as it plowed into the porch, chewing through the planks. Thr porch crumbled and Damon was swallowed by a gaping hold of splintered, upended planks.

Macklin burst out of the car and climbed over the rubble to Damon, who lay bloody and twisted amid the broken planks. Macklin grabbed the flamethrower's nozzle, put his finger on the trigger, and pressed it against Damon's mouth.

"Where's Shaw?" Macklin demanded.

Damon glared at him defiantly. "Fuck you, Macklin. Your nigger friend is going to die."

"That's not what I want to hear, Damon." Macklin grimaced. "You're going to have a very sore throat in about two seconds unless you start talking."

Damon laughed. "Kiss my ass, Macklin."

Macklin swung the nozzle away from Damon's face, aimed it at the White Wash leader's feet, and squeezed the trigger. Damon wailed in agony, his feet aflame.

"Talk," Macklin yelled over Damon's screams, planting his foot on Damon's chest so he couldn't rise.

"Shaw is buried alive, I don't know where!" he screeched. "Put out the fire!"

Macklin held the nozzle over Damon's face. "Who knows where, Damon?"

"Our Mr. Jury!" Damon cried, the fire creeping up his legs.

"Where is he?"

"A-At the Arrow." Damon wet his pants and his voice began to wither. The fire licked at Damon's belt buckle and the tanks on his back. Macklin removed his foot from Damon's chest and stepped away.

"Who is he, Damon?"

Damon raised his flaming hand over his face and stared at it in grisly fascination. "I'm dead."

Macklin dropped the nozzle and scrambled back to the car. He jumped in, slammed the door closed, and ducked under the dashboard.

The tanks ignited and Damon exploded in a fireball that burst through the flaming walls of the house and brought it crashing down on Macklin's car with a volcanic roar. The house collapsed with a fiery sigh into a towering pile of burning wood. The few surviving guards fled down the gravel road, flames licking at their heels.

A grinding sound caught their attention. They turned back and stared at the fire. Something rumbled at its core. Macklin's Cadillac blasted through the mountain of flame in a shower of cinders. The guards jumped into the brush along the roadway as the black, smoking specter tore past them, the engine growling furiously.

CHAPTER FOURTEEN

Friday, May 25, 7:45 P.M.

The doorman at the New Horizons Hotel stood aghast, his mouth gaping in shock, as Macklin's charred Cadillac rolled to a stop at the lobby doors. Macklin emerged wearing a tuxedo that nicely hid the bulge of his .44 Magnum automatic under his shoulder.

"My God, sir, what happened to your beautiful car?" the doorman asked, genuinely concerned.

Macklin dropped the keys into the doorman's open hand. "Acid rain," he mumbled, striding into the lobby and onto the express elevator to the Arrow.

A young couple, giggling and affectionate, shared the elevator with him. The couple kissed and nibbled at one another while the elevator shot upward. Macklin peered out at the glittering Los Angeles skyline and noticed the rush of the other two glass elevators that flanked his as they passed during his ascent.

The couple nuzzled their way out of the elevator when it hit the restaurant level, and Macklin rode up alone past the observation deck, office level, and finally to the ballroom, which topped the structure.

The doors slid open and Macklin slipped into the ballroom. The bustle of activity added a tangible charge that crackled through the room. Dinner was being served, and waiters scurried between the tables, delivering prime rib to the Southern California Democrats who paid $100 a plate to fête Cecil Parks.

The Arrow symbolized progress, and it was no accident that Jeffries had many of the Parks events staged here.

Macklin wound through the tables, searching faces. Somewhere was a killer waiting to strike. In the front of the room, Parks sat at a long, white-draped table chatting with powerful area Democrats. Kirk Jeffries, seated at the end of the table, spotted Macklin and shot a surprised glance at him. Macklin wandered slowly up to his friend.

"I don't want to sound unfriendly, Brett old chum, but what the hell are you doing here?" Jeffries asked in hushed tones. He narrowed his eyes on Macklin's hair. "And why does your hair look *burnt?*"

"Someone is going to make an attempt on Cecil's life tonight," Macklin whispered, hunching over and resting his hand on Jeffries's shoulder.

"What!" Jeffries exclaimed. Several heads turned along the table. Parks didn't notice. Jeffries smiled awkwardly and glanced up at Macklin. "How do you know?"

"Just trust me. We have to get Cecil out of here."

"We can't," Jeffries protested. "He still has to make his speech. These people paid a hundred dollars to see their candidate."

"They are going to see a corpse if we don't get him out of here."

"We'll call the police." Jeffries began to rise. Macklin held Jeffries down by the shoulder with a little friendly pressure.

"No," Macklin said, looking out over the crowd in front of them. "They can't be involved."

"Christ, Brett, what is it with you? Violence stalks you everywhere," he said. "Am I gonna get blown to bits every time I see you?"

The elevator on the left opened and a waiter emerged carrying a tray of empty wine glasses. Macklin squinted at him and straightened up, pulling the .44 Magnum from under his jacket.

"Don't move, scumbag!" Macklin shouted across the ballroom. It was the killer's face, the one he had seen at Burger Bob's.

The fake Mr. Jury simultaneously dropped the glasses with a crash and blasted off a shot at Macklin with a .357 Magnum. The bullet burst a vase of flowers to Macklin's left and someone screamed. Macklin aimed and panic erupted in the room. People, clamoring and running about, obscured his line of fire. Cursing, Macklin dashed through the crowd, his gun held high. Jeffries sat still at the table in stunned disbelief as pandemonium swept the room.

The elevator opened up behind the killer and people spilled out. He scrambled through them into the elevator. Macklin burst through the frantic dinner crowd just as the elevator doors were closing in front of the killer. The far right elevator door opened.

"Get out!" Macklin yelled, barreling amid the departing elevator passengers like a linebacker. He hammered the "down" button with his fist, braced his back against the cold glass to his left, and felt the elevator drop. It fell through the dark overhang of the Arrow into the twinkling night sky.

Macklin saw the flash erupt on his right and flattened himself against the door. The glass to his right shattered. The cool night wind blew into the elevator. The killer's elevator, which had stopped at one of the upper hotel floors, now disappeared as Macklin's dropped below it.

A bell clanged and Macklin's elevator stopped. The doors parted and an elderly couple wearing cowboy hats began to step in.

Macklin shoved the man in the chest with his elbow and braced himself for a shot at the killer's descending elevator. "Stand clear!" he said to them, and jammed his foot between the doors to keep it from closing and the elevator from descending.

The killer's elevator dropped into line and Macklin fired. The glass face of the other elevator crumbled and he saw the killer stumble. Perhaps a hit. The other elevator descended past him. He removed his foot and the doors slid closed. His elevator dropped. Macklin clasped a railing and hung out of the hole left by the shattered window.

Wind whipped his face. Aiming down at the killer's elevator two floors below, he squeezed the trigger. The bullets cast sparks as they glanced off the elevator's top. Macklin couldn't get a clear shot at him.

The killer's elevator stopped and Macklin closed on it. Macklin squared off for another shot. The killer fired first, the slug tearing the fabric from Macklin's left shoulder and spinning him. Macklin was about to squeeze off a shot when the express elevator, full of people, whizzed upward between the two elevators which were now descending at an equal rate.

Macklin fired the moment the express elevator was past. The bullet kicked the killer back into the railing, draping him over it like a damp towel. He was about to shoot again when the killer's elevator stopped and Macklin's continued downward to the lobby.

He holstered his .44 Magnum and dashed out of the elevator a moment later when it stopped in the lobby. He didn't want to be arrested for murder. As Macklin strode out of the lobby toward his car, he heard a woman's shrill scream and knew the impostor's elevator had come to rest.

Saturday, May 26, 11:47 A.M.

"I don't think you killed enough people yesterday," Mordente said between clenched teeth, and paced back and forth across Macklin's kitchen. "Maybe the raging forest fire you left behind you can bring the body count up a bit."

Macklin sat on the countertop in jeans and a sweat shirt, sipping a cup of coffee from a brown ceramic mug that Corinne had made him. It said DAD on it in a childish scrawl.

"Go to hell, Jessie."

Mordente froze, arched her eyebrows, and let her arms dangle limply at her sides. "What did you say?"

"You heard me," Macklin said. "And stop yelling. Sunshine is finally asleep upstairs. Or have you forgotten that those White Wash sadists raped her and kidnapped her boyfriend?"

"Fuck you, Brett. What you did yesterday was unnecessary slaughter. There were other ways to handle the situation."

"No, there wasn't," Macklin said. "Damon had to be stopped."

"Yeah, but are you any better off than before? You killed two dozen people, left a fire burning out of control, and shot up the New Horizons Hotel. We still don't know where Shaw is and that psycho may still be on the loose. The cops didn't find his body."

Mordente pulled a chair out from the kitchen table and sat down wearily. "Bravo, Mr. Jury. Bravo." She clapped her hands.

"You know, I'm getting damn sick and tired of these confrontations with you. Make up your mind about me, Jessie, and try to stick to it for a day or so, okay?"

"How can I make up my mind? With you, I'm not dealing with one person, I'm dealing with two. There's the caring father, the sensitive man, and then there's the merciless vigilante who takes lives without remorse. And you want me to deal with that?"

"I've got the same problem," Macklin said. "Part of you wants to love me, the other wants to hang me. Let me tell you something, Jessie. The only difference between you and me is that you carry a note pad and I carry a gun."

Her head fell and she wiped imaginary dirt from the table. "I'm not sure I can live with what you are." She looked up at him. "I'm not sure you can either."

"Neither of us can deal with this right now," Macklin said, slipping off the counter and standing in front of her. "My closest friend is buried alive somewhere, slowly dying if he isn't dead already. I've got to find him."

"What about the psycho?"

"Maybe some of his White Wash friends carried his corpse away," Macklin said, "and maybe he's alive. It doesn't matter right now. Cecil Parks is under heavy guard and now my only concern is finding my friend."

"So where are we going to start?" she asked, the attacking tone ebbing from her voice as fatigue crept in.

Macklin sighed and slid into the chair beside her. "I don't know."

plywood with their fingers while Shaw kicked and pushed at it from inside. They heard the screech of nails being forced and yanked the plywood face loose.

Shaw, bruised and soaking wet, fell stiffly forward into their outstretched arms. They gently held him up in a standing position. His eyes were closed and his chest heaved as he hungrily breathed in the air.

"How the hell did you survive that?" Macklin asked incredulously. Mordente was looking at Shaw as if he were a ghost.

Shaw blinked open his eyes and stretched his parched lips into a smile. "How?" He chuckled dryly and held up the index finger of his right hand. "I just jammed this in the pipe."

"The water must have washed away the loose dirt, the casket rose to the surface, and the current carried it away," she explained slowly. "Someone must be on our side. You should have drowned."

"I almost did." Shaw pulled away from them and tried standing on his own. His legs were wobbly so he wrapped his arm around Mordente's shoulder to steady himself. "But I held my breath, something happened, I stopped moving, and suddenly the water seeped out of my little box."

Macklin, the forgotten pain from his gunshot wound suddenly reasserting itself, also slipped his arm around her shoulder. With Shaw and Macklin hanging on either side of her, Mordente put her arms across their backs and led them away.

"Is it over?" Shaw asked, looking over at his injured friend.

"Yeah," Macklin said. "It's over."

EPILOGUE

The rays of the noonday sun beamed down from a cloudless sky on the lush green grass that blanketed the golf course. A fountain in the center of a pond near the ninth hole sprayed white water high into the air against a backdrop of shrubless, rocky hills. Palm trees ringed the course and provided a natural division between the healthy landscape and the barren desert beyond it.

A single, metallic red golf cart that looked like a cartoonist's caricature of a Rolls-Royce scooted down one of the tiny slopes and stopped beside a sand trap. The rake trails could still be seen in the smooth sand, not a grain of which spilled onto the putting green or the surrounding grass.

The squat, freckle-skinned old man in yellow slacks and a red, long-sleeved shirt emerged from the cart and waddled up to the golf ball lying on the rim of the putting green uphill from the hole. He adjusted his tortoiseshell glasses, firmly grasped his putter, and hunched over the ball. Staring at the ball, he saw it shake.

He straightened up and saw a plain white golf cart bouncing along the grass toward him. The man leaned on his golf club and watched the cart approach.

With an electric whine the cart glided to a stop beside the customized model. The driver wore a wrinkled flannel suit and his large brow was crinkled with emotion.

"I know who killed your grandson," Wes Craven said.

Justin Threllkiss frowned. "Who?"

"I don't know," Macklin said. "I don't know if I can take losing another person I care about."

He hung up the phone, grabbed his .44 Magnum automatic from the kitchen table, and dashed into the garage, where he loaded a shovel and a pickax into the Cadillac and drove off.

The construction site was a barren swath cut into a gentle expanse of flat land dotted with gnarly trees and knee-high weeds. Macklin drove slowly past the dirt-caked bulldozers and tractors, the white construction-office trailer, and the scattered stacks of lumber, piping, and iron bars. To his surprise, he didn't see any security guards.

He parked his car at the edge of the unfinished canal and got out. The unearthed dirt was a rich, healthy brown and lay in tiny mounds along the edge of the wide, deep gorge carved out of the soil where a river once ran. The sides of the canal were flat, blunt drops of about thirty feet and reinforced with cement pillars with wooden planks stretched between them.

A few yards away, a huge cement pipe with a six-foot-wide mouth poked out of the dirt and pointed into the canal. Macklin's eyes followed the pipe and saw that it climbed the side of a hill and disappeared, probably into the canal system that he knew lay beyond it.

Macklin walked beside the canal toward the massive pipe, scanning the land, not sure what he was looking for. Shaw could be anywhere here, and he had no idea where to begin looking. He was certain Shaw was nearby. It fit in with Damon's twisted sense of this place. The White Wash leader wanted a monument to his bloodshed, and burying Shaw here must have seemed to Damon like a good first step.

Something about the stack of scrap wood and garbage to Macklin's right caught his eye. He didn't know what, but he wasn't going to argue with instinct. Macklin walked to it and looked into the pile.

The gold wristwatch on a black-skinned arm glinted at him from the center of the pile. Macklin quickly dug through the scraps, tossing aside empty bags of cement mixer and planks of wood to get to the body underneath.

He saw the bloodstained sky-blue uniform and slowed his efforts. Lifting up a triangular sheet of soiled plywood, he looked into the dead eyes of a black security guard.

Macklin heard the gunshot before he felt it. Dumb fuck, I forgot to wear my vest, he thought to himself in that split second before the white-hot slug tore into the flesh under the right side of his rib cage. The impact lifted Macklin off his feet and tossed him backward onto the hard soil.

Bile bubbled up his throat and his mind spun, a kaleidoscope of pain and confusion, but he was aware of a person standing over his paralyzed body. He forced open his eyes and stared up the barrel of a .357 Magnum at the killer, clad in his red leather jumpsuit, a streak of black makeup over his eyes. *The impostor is still alive!*

Perspiration dotted the killer's face and Macklin knew the man was in pain. Macklin had shot him at least once at the Arrow. The impostor tossed Macklin's .44 Magnum idly away.

"Now we're both carrying lead," the man wheezed. "I could've killed you just now, you know."

Insistent waves of nausea, coupled with minor spasms in his stomach, urged Macklin to vomit. He willed it back and felt the searing pain in his side intensify twofold. Sensation, though, was beginning to return to his immovable limbs.

"You've got something to see before you die," the killer said, walking around Macklin and wrapping his free arm in a pincer grip around Macklin's neck. He dragged Macklin by the neck, painting a crimson trail in the dirt.

Each bump in the dirt sent daggers of pain cutting through Macklin's body. The warm blood seeping out of Macklin's wound felt oddly comforting as it coated the skin over his trembling stomach muscles.

The killer released Macklin beside a network of metal piping and stepped over to a large valve jutting from the pipework three feet away.

Wincing, Macklin propped himself up into a half-standing position against the pipes. A tremendous bolt of agony made him buckle. The killer leaned against the valve and trained his gun on Macklin.

Macklin saw the blood soaking through the leather jumpsuit over the killer's right shoulder and lower left side and felt a little better about his situation. The only edge the killer had on him was the gun and, judging from the wild look in his eyes and his nervous shaking, perhaps PCP pumping in his veins.

The killer motioned to the canal with a jerk of his gun. "You nigger friend is down there," he grinned.

Macklin glanced down at the canal, then back at the killer, who began to giggle.

"Watch this, Mr. Jury. You're gonna like it," he said, twisting the valve wheel with his free hand.

Macklin watched helplessly as an incredible, ground-shaking rush of water spilled out of the massive pipe twenty yards away and raged down the canal, washing away the support planks and eating away at the loose dirt.

Shaw was dead.

"Being bloated and green is better than being a nigger," the killer smirked. "I just did your buddy a favor."

Macklin flung himself at the killer, grabbing for the gun. The killer shrieked and drove his fist into Macklin's wound. Macklin screamed and fell away, hitting the ground and rolling onto his back, squirming with pain.

"Shitface, ass-sucking, nigger-loving, son of a bitch," the killer whispered hoarsely, and jabbed the gun barrel at Macklin's damp forehead. "Death to your kind."

Macklin heard the explosion of a gunshot to his right. The bullet slammed into the killer's chest and stood him straight up, his mouth gaping open and his eyes wide. The eyes stared down at Macklin and he leveled his gun at Macklin's face again.

Another gunshot rang out. The killer's forehead split open and blood dribbled out in a thick, globby stream. Macklin propped himself up on his elbows and watched the killer fall to his knees. A huff of sour air hissed out of the killer's mouth like escaping helium from a balloon and then he toppled face forward and slapped into the dirt beside Macklin.

Gravel crunched behind Macklin, and Jessica Mordente appeared beside him, his .44 Magnum held firmly in her hand. They looked at each other and he saw a familiar cold emptiness in her eyes. He had seen it before, what seemed like a long time ago, in his own mirror-reflected eyes. Now she too was a vigilante.

She kicked the killer over on his back with her foot and stared down at him with disgust.

"It's Justin Threllkiss," she muttered.

"Threllkiss?" Macklin said, glancing at the bloody face. "Threllkiss is an old man."

She nodded weakly. "This is his grandson, Justin Threllkiss the Third, his only living heir."

Macklin frowned and tried to stand. Mordente shoved the gun into the waistband of her slacks and helped Macklin to his feet.

"Can you stand?" she asked.

Macklin nodded and looked over his shoulder at the water rushing down the canal. He had failed. Another loved one was claimed by the disease. Leaning against the pipes, he examined his wound for the first time. It looked as though the bullet had passed right through him.

"What about Shaw?" She stood at the canal's edge, looking down at the torrent of water. Her voice was flat and emotionless.

Macklin hobbled to the valve. "He's down there." Together, Macklin and Mordente turned the valve and shut off the flow of water. It was a hopeless gesture, but somehow it seemed like the right thing to do. The water thinned out and they could see the ravaged soil peeking through.

"You need to see a doctor, Brett. You're bleeding awfully bad."

Macklin slipped his arm around her shoulder. "Yeah, let's go."

Slowly, they made their way to Macklin's car. He fell against the hood, breathing heavily, his face flushed and wet from the exertion and pain.

"I'll follow your car out of here," he said.

"You can't drive, Brett. You can barely stand," she protested. "You're liable to pass out on the road."

"We've got no choice," he said hoarsely, his throat dry and raw. "We can't leave a car here. We can't be connected with this."

Mordente knew he was right. "Okay, I'll go to my car and be back here in a sec."

He felt as if he were on fire, the flames from his bullet wound scorching the rest of his skin. Macklin crawled into his car and sagged in the driver's seat. Drowsiness fogged his eyes. Macklin blinked hard and twisted the ignition. The engine grumbled to life.

Mordente's Mazda RX-7 pulled out in front of him, and Macklin jerked the gear into drive and followed her down the tree-lined dirt roadway. He held on to the wheel tightly and gritted against the pain each jostling bump of the roadway caused.

They had driven less than half a mile when Macklin saw Mordente's brake lights flash on and her car stop. Mordente got out and walked back to Macklin's car. He rolled down the window.

"The road is washed out," she said, grimacing. "We're going to have to walk from here."

"Shit," Macklin groaned, throwing open the door. He got out and stomped past Mordente and into the trees. Anger, he discovered, blunted the pain. The water had settled into a huge pond where the current had washed out the roadway. She fell into step beside him. Silently, they walked around the water-torn roadway and then followed the watery landscape.

She reached her left arm across his back and held him firmly under the left shoulder. Macklin smiled at her and put his right arm around her shoulder, using her for support. He felt as if they were the last two people on earth, and he wouldn't have been surprised if the ground suddenly opened under their feet and swallowed them up.

Mordente slowed.

"What's the matter?" Macklin asked, concerned but thankful for the rest.

"Listen," she whispered.

Macklin concentrated. At first he only noticed the stillness of the valley and the trickle of water in the muddy dirt beside them. Then he noticed the thumping. It sounded distant and muted, like someone punching a pillow.

The sound was ahead of them and across the muddy divide. Mordente and Macklin, without discussing it, plodded through the mud and water downstream toward the sound.

The closer they got, the more distinct the pounding became. It was frantic and insistent. Macklin squinted into the trees and bushes ahead but saw nothing. His curiosity made him forget the pain just a bit. It was still there, but it wasn't immobilizing him.

Mordente stumbled and Macklin pressed ahead a few feet, looking back to make sure she was okay. He rounded an outcropping of brush and then stopped, frozen with surprise.

"What is it, Brett?" Mordente said, coming up behind him.

Macklin began to smile. A plywood casket with a narrow pipe jutting out of it stood upright in the mud like a signpost, water spilling out of its seams.

"Ronny," Macklin shouted. "Are you all right?"

"Just get me out of here," Shaw replied weakly.

Macklin scrambled to the casket, his pain overwhelmed by his relief that his friend was alive. He and Mordente pried the plywood with their fingers while Shaw kicked and pushed at it from inside. They heard the screech of nails being forced and yanked the plywood face loose.

Shaw, bruised and soaking wet, fell stiffly forward into their outstretched arms. They gently held him up in a standing position. His eyes were closed and his chest heaved as he hungrily breathed in the air.

"How the hell did you survive that?" Macklin asked incredulously. Mordente was looking at Shaw as if he were a ghost.

Shaw blinked open his eyes and stretched his parched lips into a smile. "How?" He chuckled dryly and held up the index finger of his right hand. "I just jammed this in the pipe."

"The water must have washed away the loose dirt, the casket rose to the surface, and the current carried it away," she explained slowly. "Someone must be on our side. You should have drowned."

"I almost did." Shaw pulled away from them and tried standing on his own. His legs were wobbly so he wrapped his arm around Mordente's shoulder to steady himself. "But I held my breath, something happened, I stopped moving, and suddenly the water seeped out of my little box."

Macklin, the forgotten pain from his gunshot wound suddenly reasserting itself, also slipped his arm around her shoulder. With Shaw and Macklin hanging on either side of her, Mordente put her arms across their backs and led them away.

"Is it over?" Shaw asked, looking over at his injured friend.

"Yeah," Macklin said. "It's over."

EPILOGUE

The rays of the noonday sun beamed down from a cloudless sky on the lush green grass that blanketed the golf course. A fountain in the center of a pond near the ninth hole sprayed white water high into the air against a backdrop of shrubless, rocky hills. Palm trees ringed the course and provided a natural division between the healthy landscape and the barren desert beyond it.

A single, metallic red golf cart that looked like a cartoonist's caricature of a Rolls-Royce scooted down one of the tiny slopes and stopped beside a sand trap. The rake trails could still be seen in the smooth sand, not a grain of which spilled onto the putting green or the surrounding grass.

The squat, freckle-skinned old man in yellow slacks and a red, long-sleeved shirt emerged from the cart and waddled up to the golf ball lying on the rim of the putting green uphill from the hole. He adjusted his tortoiseshell glasses, firmly grasped his putter, and hunched over the ball. Staring at the ball, he saw it shake.

He straightened up and saw a plain white golf cart bouncing along the grass toward him. The man leaned on his golf club and watched the cart approach.

With an electric whine the cart glided to a stop beside the customized model. The driver wore a wrinkled flannel suit and his large brow was crinkled with emotion.

"I know who killed your grandson," Wes Craven said.

Justin Threllkiss frowned. "Who?"

"Brett Macklin, a Los Angeles charter-airline pilot. He's also Mr. Jury."

Craven thought he saw Threllkiss nod, or perhaps it was just the old man's palsy shake. Threllkiss hunched over the ball, glanced at the hole, then down at the ball again.

Threllkiss tapped the ball gently with his putter. The ball rolled slowly down the green, circled the hole once, then fell in with a clunk.

"Brett Macklin will come to know tremendous suffering," Justin Threllkiss said, "and then he will die."

AFTERWORD

The creation of Brett Macklin—and "Ian Ludlow"—is explained in this essay, published as a "My Turn" column in Newsweek magazine in 1985. Pinnacle Books went out of business before the fourth novel in the series was set to be published.

HOT SEX, GORY VIOLENCE

How One Student Earns Course Credit and Pays Tuition

My name is Ian Ludlow. Well, not really. But that's the name on my four *.357 Vigilante* adventures that Pinnacle Books will publish this spring. Most of the time I'm Lee Goldberg, a mild-mannered UCLA senior majoring in mass communications and trying to spark a writing career at the same time. It's hard work. I haven't quite achieved a balance between my dual identities of college student and hack novelist.

The adventures of Mr. Jury, a vigilante into doing the LAPD's dirty work, are often created in the wee hours of the night, when I should be studying, meeting my freelance-article deadlines, or, better yet, sleeping. More often than not, my nocturnal writing spills over into my classes the next morning. Brutal fistfights, hot sexual encounters, and gory violence are frequently scrawled across my anthropology notes or written amid my professor's insights on Whorf's hypothesis. Students sitting next to me who glance at my lecture notes are shocked to see notations like "Don't move, scumbag, or I'll wallpaper the room with your brains."

I once wrote a pivotal rape scene during one of my legal-communications classes, and I'm sure the girl who sat next to me thought I was a psychopath. During the first half of the lecture, she kept looking with wide eyes from my notes to my face as if my nose were melting onto my binder or something. At the break she disappeared, and I didn't see her again the rest of the quarter. My professors, though, seem pleased to see me sitting in the back of the classroom writing furiously. I guess they think I'm hanging on their every word. They're wrong.

I've tried to lessen the strain between my conflicting identities by marrying the two. Through the English department, I'm getting academic credit for the books. That amazes my grandpa Cy, who can't believe there's a university crazy enough to reward me for writing "lots of filth." The truth is, it's writing and it's learning, and it's getting me somewhere. Just where, I'm not sure. My grandpa Cy thinks it's going to get me the realization I should join him in the furniture business.

I don't admit to many people that I'm writing books. It sounds so pompous, arrogant, and phony when you say that in Los Angeles. See, everybody in Los Angeles is writing a book or screenplay. Walk into any 7-Eleven, tell the clerk you're an agent or a producer, and he'll whip out a handwritten, 630-page epic he's been keeping under the register for a chance like this.

I do involve my closest friends in the secret world of Ian Ludlow. When I finished writing my first sex scene, I made six copies and passed them around for a critique. I felt like I was distributing pornography. "How do you compliment a sex scene?" a girl I know complained. "It's embarrassing." Another friend rewrote the scene so it sounded like a cross between a beating and extensive surgery.

Among my family and even my friends, I find myself constantly apologizing for what I'm doing. Maybe I wouldn't if I were writing a Larry McMurtry or John Updike book. But I know what this is. This is a black cover with a rugged hero in the forefront, shoving a massive gun into the reader's face. I feign disgust, mutter something about "a guy's got to break in somehow," and quickly change the subject.

But the truth is, it's fun. And since Ian Ludlow is the guy who will take the heat for it, I can let myself relax and enjoy it. I'm building on those childhood hours spent in front of my mom's ancient Smith Corona, banging out hokey tales about superspies and supervillains. My work is still hokey, except now someone is paying me for it. And paying me not badly, either. I can pay for a whole year of college from the advances for the four novels.

The opportunity came my way thanks to Lewis Perdue, a journalism professor who writes those bulky conspiracy thrillers and harbors dreams of being the next Robert Ludlum. I used to read his manuscripts and debate the merits of Lawrence Sanders and Ken Follett. Then, when Pinnacle asked him to do an "urban man's action-adventure series," he passed it on to me. Pretty soon I was buying books like *The Butcher*, *The Executioner*, *The Penetrator*, *The Destroyer*, and *The Terminator* by the armful and flipping through the latest issues of *Soldier of Fortune* and *Gung-Ho*. After a week or two of wading through this, I was ready to spill blood across my home computer screen.

There's a part of me that doesn't like what I'm doing. It lectures me while I'm making some bad guy eat hot lead. It tells me I should be writing a novel about relationships and feelings, about the problems my peers are facing. *I will*, I say to myself, *later. There's plenty of time.*

ABOUT THE AUTHOR

Lee Goldberg is a two-time Edgar Award and two-time Shamus Award nominee and the #1 *New York Times* best-selling author of more than forty novels, including the *Eve Ronin* series, fifteen *Monk* novels, eight *Diagnosis Murder* novels, and five novels co-authored with Janet Evanovich. He has also written and/or produced many TV shows, including *Diagnosis Murder*, *SeaQuest*, and *Monk*, and he is the cocreator of the *Mystery 101* series of Hallmark movies. As an international television consultant, he has advised networks and studios in Canada, France, Germany, Spain, China, Sweden, and the Netherlands on the creation, writing, and production of episodic television series. He's also the founder of the publishing companies Brash Books and Cutting Edge Books. You can find more information about Lee and his work at www.leegoldberg.com.

www.ingramcontent.com/pod-product-compliance
Lightning Source LLC
Chambersburg PA
CBHW031240260626
47169CB00007B/2384